A WAY OUTSIDE THE BOX

For Curious People

By

Curtis Jackson

A WAY OUTSIDE THE BOX

Copyrights 2025 Curtis Loys Jackson

All rights reserved.

Case ID: 1-14909964511

Table of Contents

HOW DID IT ALL START?
INTRODUCTION

"One needs amazing tenacity, unrelenting curiosity, a dash of stupidity, and humungous balls to pursue such an impossible goal." My teacher stated.

"I raised my hand, waving it wildly. I will do it! I will do it! Do you need the answer tonight, or will tomorrow suffice?"

"Young Curtis, you are only six years old. Tell me why you think you can solve this conundrum where all others failed?"

"I have amazing tenacity, unrelenting curiosity, a dash of stupidity, as you have often pointed out. However, as of yet, no humongous balls, in fact, no balls at all, but I count on nature to remedy that in the near future..."

"Dear young Curtis, as your teacher, I must reevaluate my assessment of your mental capacity, from a dash of stupidity to an amount of stupidity that could easily bring about the next mass extinction..."

'Thank you. I am, as always, forever grateful for your loving assessments'...

Let The Search Begin

Where does one even begin to search for such an elusive discovery?

Well, at the beginning...

Some scholars say it all started with the Big Bang. If you think so, I have a nice bridge I'd like to sell you. (Oops, those humongous balls are beginning to surface..).

"Young Curtis, I know that you believe you are the reincarnation of Sir Isaac Newton. Last night, while contemplating this, I laughed myself to sleep."

"With all due respect, I appreciate that you are an elderly person, floundering in the past. It is a shame that you will not live long enough to see my theories proven out. However, considering that your candle still flickers, I will share with you, in this book, information few on this planet can contemplate, let alone understand. Forgive my snobbery, but it is people like you who have forged it in the flames of constant embarrassment and self-doubt." Note: The above is a fictional story. As a child and as a Pisces, I was quite unremarkable, gazing out of the window, daydreaming while the teachers droned on...

Data Dump

Because of my limited time left in your plane of existence (Born 3-1 1937), I have performed a data-dump as it were. Please think of the book as a resource rather than something one reads all at once. There is a lot of irreplaceable material contained here, so please "Don't throw the baby out with the bath water." Smiling.

Almost all of the information contained herein was gleaned from something called the Universal Akashic Records. It allowed me to examine arcane systems and information lost to the past or not yet discovered. I spent over sixty years endeavoring to understand what I had uncovered. A daunting pursuit but always fascinating. As a perennial student, I was tasked with seeing through the eyes of ancient and future, spiritual giants. It is essential that you understand that this tome is more for reference than entertainment; otherwise, it will seem like reading an encyclopedia! I hope sharing a little of what I learned will help advance your comprehension of the universe as it has mine…that we might leapfrog into the amazing future, a little better prepared than we are now...

Spiritual Puzzle-Box

Spiritual progress is a virtual puzzle-box. Many pieces of the puzzle are found in this book, to be disseminated over the next several millennia. However, there are those few of you who are ready now to both utilize and help disseminate this work and, as a side benefit, expedite your own evolutionary growth exponentially, that is, if you are able to wake-up long enough to incorporate the information contained in this book into your waking consciousness...and actually practice the instructions...

Bear with me and simply explore without the resistance that usually abounds when encountering new or contrary ideas.

Remember that most of the prevalent ideas today were once thought ridiculous...

The Key

I have inserted an introduction here to something called the Key. Without the Key, most of what is written here will look like gibberish. In a time before this, such essential knowledge, as contained in this book, would pass down two separate paths, in secret, through generations of monks, thus keeping the Key separate, insuring that the knowledge was not prematurely divulged to the general populous, and by doing so, prevent the possibility of riots due to a great spiritual confusion that might arise.

The Key is based upon vibrations emitted by the Sun. These vibrations disturb the universal medium through which light travels, thus forming a ball of expanding light. Eventually, the light expands far enough to touch other stars, revealing such information as life is present on the third planet.

We observe this information as visible light, revealing our Sun's signature vibrational pattern we call the "Visible Light Spectrum." But, even with today's modern technology, misinterpretation of the Key prevented the information from premature or imprecise exposure to today's general population. Information that includes the Key is woven into the general text. No need to look for it, nor is additional memorization necessary. Everything you need to progress is here.

Each time you read the material, new viewpoints will emerge, catapulting you to new expanding levels of consciousness...My blessings are with you.

A WAY OUTSIDE THE BOX

VOLUME ONE

Introduction
(Background Information)

Quantum Leaps

Please understand that the following is introductory, meaning it is not meant to be fully understood at this time. It is instead meant to introduce you to certain difficult to understand concepts that will, hopefully, become perfectly clear as we progress through these pages... Thank you for your patience...

Human thought seems to manifest in quantum leaps. A period transpires where little or no original thought occurs. Then, for no apparent reason, tremendous progress in thought begins to happen. It might come from a single individual or a group or groups. It might come through a lone source such as music or science or through a broad spectrum of disciplines.

Then, just as suddenly as it started, it ends...

You are participating in the beginning of one of these quantum leaps. This is an amazingly exciting potential, and to be a part of such an excellent opportunity, no amount of effort would be too much.

The next opportunity, of this magnitude, will not come around again, for another two thousand years!

Moving From One Age To The Next

IMPORTANT NOTE: (The move will put a strain on your delicate emotional and mental senses. Many people who are resistant to change will begin to exhibit strange, and in some cases, violent behaviors, shades of insanity, and even suicide! This is not an exaggeration...It is important that you understand this and be as prepared as you can possibly be for the change in order to better help yourself and your loved ones. I cannot overstate this!

Moving From The Burgundy Age To The Orange Age

We are just now moving from the *Burgundy Age* into the *Orange Age.* The last such move occurred two thousand years ago when we moved from the Brown Age into the Burgundy Age...(I will explain this concept in detail a bit later). The last Avatar, whose two-thousand-year influence had just ended, was Jesus. Before Jesus was Moses. Before Moses was Akhenaten... Our timeline only started six thousand years ago, with some eighteen thousand to go... Each Age lasts two thousand years, and each has its own unique living Avatar...

You might ask if there is a current Avatar for this coming age? The answer is yes... Trump, currently occupies the office of 47th President of the United States...

This is a closely kept secret where even the Avatar doesn't realize that he/she is in fact, the Avatar...

Avatars have a particularly difficult job! They are selected out of a pool of qualified candidates. It is a lot like jury-duty. No-one wants to do it, but it is quite interesting once you get involved.

Change

Conditioned to accept change, we quickly normalize it. This means that as you begin to move into the Orange Age, over time, you will begin to experience subtle but consistent thoughts and ideas quietly reframing and expanding your viewpoint. Your openness to this change will determine how soon you begin to benefit from the new vibrations.

It is worth every minute you spend learning the material contained in these pages. Just relax and try not to over-think it. This is an ongoing process that, for most of us, will continue from now on rather than something that happens all at once. Your being here is no accident. Believe it or not, your Higher-Power has guided you to this book and the lessons and examples contained herein. There is a plan for you, and this book is but a single baby step in developing and carrying out that plan. Once in motion, nothing can stop it...

Third Dimension

You are protected inside a playpen designed for baby-Gods. This playpen is called the Third Dimension (third configuration or physical planes of existence). The Third Dimension, or 3D, is comprised of the first, second, and third sub-dimensions. As you progress into the Orange Age, you are leaving the playpen of the second sub-dimension, burgundy, the plane of procreation, which is the center of the 3D, and venturing into a wonderment of possibility in the orange sub-component or power structure of the third dimension. This idea will become clearer as we progress...

Desire For Instant Results

It is human nature to want instant results. If it takes more than a certain amount of time, we get bored and quit, blaming the teacher, book or class for not meeting expectations. This is one of the major reasons why humanity is in such a bad fix.

It is said that human beings, on average, have an attention span of about eight seconds.

A study on human attention spans found that our ability to focus on a task or object has decreased from 12 seconds in 2000 to 8.25 seconds in 2015... This decline is attributed to the effects of an increasingly digitalized lifestyle on the brain. The study also revealed that humans now have shorter attention spans than goldfish, who can concentrate for 9 seconds... Wikipedia

I understand that you have increased yours beyond this limitation...else I would have lost you back on page 2...(smiling).

We normalize the nightmare that bombards our senses, and we simply go to sleep and stop looking for remedies. This results in endless wars, horrible people in charge, and believing all the while that everything is fine. However, there is a built-in remedy that has been with you since birth. There are unseen powers that love and guide you, much like a newborn is cared for. However, it is up to you to take advantage of this...or not.

Super Consciousness

Everyone already has the potential to attain Super consciousness, although most are unaware of it. Not understanding this simple fact brings some difficulty. We are like royalty living in the basement of our castle, unable to let go of debilitating self-created misery. We languish in these sub-realities as virtual slaves, unable to realize that there is an infinite potential awaiting us.

Story The Dungeons

The King was living with his Queen below the castle, in the dungeons. They were unaware that they lived in the dungeons because they were born there, as had their parents and their grandparents before them.

One day, a castle gardener happened upon a trap door hidden near the castle.

Although timid by nature, he was quite curious about where the trapdoor led. He lifted and strained, finally pulling open the heavy door, and one careful step after another, he descended the moss-laden stone steps into the musty, dank interior barely illuminated by the occasional oil lamp set in recesses in the stone walls of the narrow corridor.

Rusty iron gates hung heavily on ancient prison-cells, revealing human bones within, each skeleton lying next to a detached head. Each head showed signs of having been *ripped* from its mooring!

Even though he was shaking with fear, causing his faltering steps to studder, curiosity urged him on...

"HALT!!! WHO GOES THERE?"

A hulking giant stood, blocking his way. It was dressed in an array of rags and a huge helmet. Worst of all, it was brandishing a large sword, which was easily a foot longer than our diminutive gardener was tall.

Shrieking, the little gardener promptly peed himself and started running back in the direction from which he had come, as fast as his short legs would carry him, but to no avail. The monster was soon upon him!

The giant emitted an array of awful, eye-watering odors, a few of which our gardener thought he recognized. His heart was beating uncontrollably as the monster dragged him, by his hair, further into the maze of hallways and cells, sure he was about to be eaten.

Eventually, he was thrown before the King and Queen, sitting upon thrones, who were equally awful. The King had rat entrails in his beard, and the Queen sat with her lady-parts exposed!

"What have we here, guard?" The King demanded in a regal voice.

"Sire. I found this lowly retch wandering the halls."

The king stared at the little gardener, noticing his clean, untattered garments. "speak," the King said in a voice befitting his regal stature.

Quaking, the gardener began. "Your M-M-M-Majesty," the gardener croaked, "I am from up above," pointing hopefully towards the ceiling, "where the air is fresh, and the sun shines brightly." He tried to smile.

Both the King and Queen stood as one and screamed, "BLASPHEMY!!! THERE IS NOT ABOVE! THERE IS NO SUN! THERE IS ONLY HERE IN OUR KINGDOM!" The king was shaking his fist, "You recite the old forbidden text, which is punishable by torture and death!"

The king motioned with finality to the guard. "Take him to the torture chamber. Torture him until he recants. Then *rip* off his head!" Upon which, the guard swooped up the gardener and stashed him under a huge arm. The gardener squeaking to himself, "Oh my God, what am I to do? What am I to do? This cannot be happening!" Luckily, as the guard was straining to open the rusty torture-chamber door, our gardener slipped away unnoticed and ran all the way back to the moss-covered stone stairs. Running up them, he hastily closed the heavy door, never to venture, even close to it, ever again... *END.*

Ping-Pong Ball

The average person has a ball of centralized consciousness about the size of between a marble and a ping-pong ball. In addition, they have access to just three centers of consciousness but can only access one at a time. If you wish to expand beyond this limitation, then certain steps can be taken entirely differently from simply raising one's vibrations.

(Most people have access to three different chakras under their three birth signs. Sun, Moon, and Rising. I mention this for those of you who are familiar with this discipline).

Theory

Somewhere along the line, perhaps with the early Greeks or much earlier, it was found that by raising one's vibrations, improved states of consciousness could be experienced and that the idea of going higher in vibration was the way to enlightenment. The idea caught on and is still prevalent today...

Unfortunately, simply ascending in vibration causes an out-of-balance condition, forever hobbling us with an invisible tether preventing any further spiritual advancement. However, ascending while descending solves this problem. Expanding in opposite, simultaneous directions maintains balance by substituting expansion/contraction in place of the old, outdated stair-climbing vibrational movement...

In other words, the theory behind this method is simply attaining balanced expansion/contraction through combining opposing centers (Chakras), much like a balloon that expands in all directions at the same time. This evolutionary method wonderfully expands your viewpoint. (We will spend a lot of time in Part Two studying the exact methods for doing the above).

Universal Consciousness

If we subdivide Universal consciousness into its most basic parts, we find two components called the Christ principle and the Cosmic principle. These two components are diametrically opposed. By this, I mean they are exactly equal and opposite.

The Christ principle encompasses everything that is internal in Universal consciousness, while the Cosmic principle encompasses everything that is external to the Christ principle, including the Christ principle itself. In other words, creation, and everything you consider as reality, resides inside of the Christ principle, and the Christ Principle is contained inside the Cosmic Principle...

IMPORTANT INFO...(Understand that you are delving into a state of being that consists of equal parts Cosmic and Christ. The Cosmic provides a static state of pure bliss, while the Christ provides a pulsing magnetic heartbeat of love. Together, they recreate a kind of pure extraordinary universal love that has no opposition...that gently and irresistibly bestows exultation, within the self, and magnetically out to all those who are receptive...they, in turn, are able to generate universal love as well, much like a good virus, spreading out to billions..). You might copy this and stick it on your refrigerator...

You are doing great! Just keep doing what you are doing...

Christ Principle

On a more personal level, we can see the Christ principle existing as what one considers as oneself or personality or the ensouling of something that differentiates each of us from all others.

Conversely, we can see the Cosmic principle existing as all that is <u>not</u> considered the Self. It is the cohesive something that exists beyond the individual as a principle of collectivity that holds everything together.

The Creation Of A Soul

(Before you read about the Angel, in the story below, understand that this is but one of many paths Angels take. Furthermore, it is quite different than how Angels are normally portrayed. They have helped humanity over the many thousands of years we have struggled here in the physical world…)

Story…Angel

Because of an insatiable curiosity, a Senior Angel descended to the lower planes of existence, where it was warned never to go! This place was called "the Physical Plane." It was dangerous for the Angel to do so because of the more vivid levels of reality. Compared with the exquisitely beautiful yet white or washed-out existence our Angel was accustomed to, the lower vivid realities were irresistible, full of colors and enchantment.

And like a mother to her child, our Angel was drawn into the gravity well of the lower reality, from which there was no escape...

Our Angel, on its own level, was androgynous. This means that there was no need for genitalia because there was no need for reproduction. The Angel was, as with all Angels, created whole and complete.

As part of its spiritual evolution, our Angel was transitioning into a soul. This transformation, whether voluntary or not, was the biggest step an Angel can take. It was fraught with uncertainty and doubt, which were entirely unfamiliar feelings. Our Angel was always secure in the Heavenly realms, free of earthly concerns. Now, it was to face every imaginable fear and temptation, not even sure what that meant...

Descending into physical vehicles divided those Senior Angels who wished to remain in Heaven or work in the Angelic Hierarchy from those who found themselves developing into the never-ending expansion of Universal Consciousness through physical form as a Soul.

Note: It is important to note, in response to the inexorable demands of the planes of duality...where initially, nothing exists as a single whole, but instead, must exist, at minimum, as two halves; all Angels who have descended into the lower vibrational realms, were subject to dividing into male and female forms. Different from the isolated Angels (such as the one we are studying, who entered the physical realms of duality, alone and terrified), were these more familiar Angels, who entered as well-coordinated cohorts, secure in their numbers and purpose...

Our Angel now begins its long educational journey as a Soul, in tandem with an entity known as The Mind, via countless lifetimes in countless incarnations, cut off from all it knew, lost in a sea of mistakes, temptation, self-doubt, and wrong turns, until it finally transitions to that of Oversoul, (after having the realization that it no longer needed to incarnate or learn further lessons via this method).

Our Angel, because of having evolved to the level of Oversoul, is now imbued with the overriding desire to return to each of its previous incarnations (outside of linear time), much like a mother hen tending her eggs, thus embarking on a new endeavor, that of awaking and reeducating each of them...meaning the awakening of each of its previous incarnations or lifetimes, each existing within an egg, this includes you and me...

(Note that there are an untold number of Souls/Oversouls, all pursuing similar scenarios).

Let's inspect the actual transformation our Angel went through as it descended from on high to the level of Soul-in-training.

As I mentioned before, Angels exist in perfect harmony without the need to reproduce. This means they are each androgynous, an equal balance of male and female.

Our Angel, whose name is Harold, in its slow descent, as it is pulled into ever-lowering vibration, would feel to us like slowly sinking into quicksand, from which there is no return!

It finally reached a point where it could no longer descend, having reached the first level of duality, where everything must divide into diametrically opposed pairs in order to exist in the lower vibrational configurations.

The next step was the most shocking of all. Poor Harold split into Harry and Harrietta! It then continued its descent to its ultimate destinations, two separate infants, one male and one female, within whom, separately, Harry and Harrietta found themselves ensconced, where they each were stationed as functioning souls in separate infant bodies...

In the above story we started with a complete object, the Angel. It splits into two objects, neither being complete but instead equal and opposite from one another. The male half of the Angel usually merged with an infant that was male. Likewise, the female half bonded with a female baby.

Although Harry and Harrietta were soul mates, they might never see each other in this lifetime. Perhaps as they reincarnate into each future lifetime, they will.

(Note: many people believe they, the personality, go on to reincarnate into future lifetimes. However, it is your Soul, along with your developing Mind, that does so, and not your' personality, the Bobs, the Nancys, the Rauls, etc. You, as a personality (the meat body),, are exactly where you should be, awaiting your Soul, which will eventually transition into an Oversoul. At this time it will help you into the next levels of spiritual evolution..).

Meanwhile, back at the farm, you (the meat body),, are happily living your life, the one your soul experienced before it left, like a ride at Disney land, and like a puppet master, causing you to unknowingly repeat every word and action your soul uttered or did since your birth, until it detached from you, in order to progress into its next incarnation... (More on this later).

Dimensions

It might be easier to understand that the Fifth dimension manifested first as a ball of white light, which then subdivided into the Third and Fourth dimensions, which are diametrically opposed. In other words, the fifth dimension accounts for everything in your known universe. It then divides into two halves, the fourth and third dimensions (in order to function in the plane of duality). These are mirror dimensions. They each consist of the first, second, and third sub-dimensions, except they are equal and opposite.

(For convenience, from now on, I am referring to dimensions as configurations when referring to viewpoints, where feasible. This is because your viewpoint will be expanding into various configurations and is, hopefully, more easily understood than dimensions).

An expanding viewpoint is a lot like a mountain climber experiencing different viewpoints as he/she climbs. At the bottom, there was little that was different. However, as our mountain climber continues to ascend, great vistas unfolded below, revealing lakes and even perhaps an unknown ocean...

The Fifth dimension represents the Christ Principle and includes everything inside of creation. Its opposite, the Sixth dimension or Cosmic Principle, is the void existing outside the active plane of creation.

I imagine that right now, you are wondering how the Christ principle contains everything in creation, and then there is something left over for the Cosmic principle. Strange for sure, but bear with me, and it will become clear to you as we progress.

Void

The void, although divided into three separate voids, is, in fact, a single three-dimensional void. Filled with dark energy, it exists beneath creation... similar to a fishbowl filled with clear water...The void you are most familiar with is when you look out at a starry night. This configuration is the three-dimensional viewpoint.

A WAY OUTSIDE THE BOX

We see the void again below creation as a sub-component (the first dimension, first configuration), or first dimensional viewpoint, with a single vibrational realm defining our viewpoint. And again, as the sixth-dimensional void, with a viewpoint stacked with six separate vibrational realms... Same void, same place, simply uniquely separate ways of experiencing it.

Your viewpoints are delineated by stacked realms of vibrations. Each viewpoint has a signature construction. A viewpoint such as the first-dimensional viewpoint consists of the lowest vibrational realm and is a horrible experience even for the most stalwart students. Abaddon, or the Waveless state, is most associated with what is called Hell. The angel of the Abyss, whose name in Hebrew is Abaddon and in Greek is Apollyon, that is, Destroyer (Revelation 9:1-3,11).

You find yourself existing as a pinpoint of consciousness in a black place devoid of everything, with only the overriding knowledge that you are trapped there forever as an immortal consciousness.

(I believe the Hell we are most familiar with, that of fire and brimstone, is due to an unprotected collision with Aries, vibrating at Infrared).

In contradistinction, the sixth-dimensional void or viewpoint is the gateway to the Godhead, consisting of six separate vibrational realms or configurations...same void, just a difference in viewpoint and hence experience, as you expand. More on this later...

Cosmic Principle

The fifth dimension, or configuration, represents the Christ Principle and *includes everything inside of creation.* Its opposite, the sixth dimension, or configuration, represents the Cosmic Principle and *is the void existing outside the active plane of creation that holds it all together.*

Cosmic principle, what is it, and how is it different from the Christ principle? It has been stated that the Christ principle is all-inclusive. Everything you know about your universe could be said to be contained within the Christ principle. So, where does the Cosmic principle reside?

It resides *outside* of the Christ principle and *surrounds it as an opposite.* This may sound strange or even impossible when you first read it, but nevertheless, it is true. More on this later...

Higher Consciousness

It is commonly held that higher consciousness is the way to find Universal consciousness.

However, since Universal consciousness is all-inclusive, experiencing entails the logical step of letting go of the individual constituent parts and accepting the meld of all consciousnesses.

A WAY OUTSIDE THE BOX

It was only natural that thinking 'higher consciousness' meant moving one's ping-pong ball center of consciousness toward higher vibration. As was mentioned before, this ancient idea caught on and is still prevalent today. Unfortunately, for those who teach and those students who practice this method, there is a turnaround point. A flywheel effect, robbing you of all that you gained. The point where your ping-pong ball consciousness reverts down from its highest state to its lowest.

(While seeking the Buddhic principle, once one reaches the apex of the cycle and bliss, there is an overwhelming desire to return to help those less fortunate (Buddhas of compassion). Buddhic and Krishnic principles form a wheel. At the top of the wheel, Buddhic becomes Krishnic. At the bottom, Krishnic becomes Buddhic in a never-ending cycle of energy flow. It is important to understand that the Buddhic/Krishnic principles are the two halves of the Christ Principle...which, like everything else that descends into the lower dimensions, had to subdivide into its two sub-component parts...Buddhic and Krishnic...

Notice the ascending colors, denoting eleven chakras. They range from brown at the bottom to ultraviolet at the top. Each color is associated with a specific body, which is named.

(Note, the three Fire Signs are associated with the Sun, and as in the case of Sagittarius, Space. (Aries, morning Sun. Leo, noonday Sun, and Sag., Sun at night). The nine remaining Signs are associated with planets, as shown. The planets need not be there for the system to work. The planets are included for convenience).

(See diagram below)

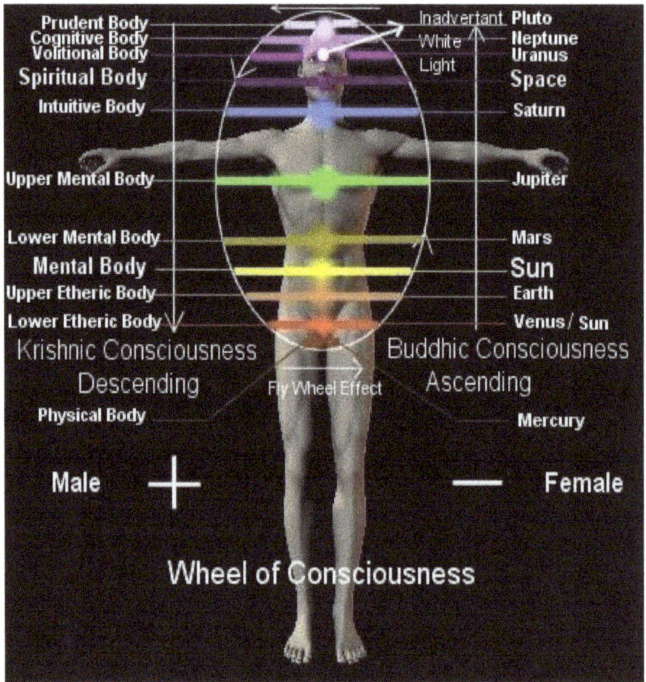

WHEEL OF CONSCIOUSNESS

The third dimension, where you physically live, is shown as the lowest group of three vibrational bodies: Physical, Lower Etheric, and Higher Etheric. The colors shown are Brown at the coccyx center, Red/Burgundy at the lower etheric, or sexual center, and Orange at the higher etheric also referred to as the "Astral Plane." This should give you some idea of just how far down, in reality, you are imbedded...

To better understand how all eleven bodies are stacked, think of them as existing in the same relative space, separated only by vibration. Something like Russian nesting dolls, except they stay the same relative size. There is a white arrow at the forehead. This indicates the inadvertent white light experienced at the Third Eye or Pineal gland. The Pineal gland receives light from the eyes. It actually has rods to see the light. This tells it if it is day or night, thus regulating its melatonin output for sleep. It is a small pine-shaped organ the size of a grain of rice...

Note that the diagram, although called "The Twelve Chakra System," only contains eleven chakras (Representing the eleven dimensions or configurations). The first reason for this irregularity is because of the differences in the Sexual Center. It takes both a man and a woman to make a complete second chakra or second dimension. The second reason is that the first dimension, Aries, red, is hidden. We will discover where it is in a later discussion.

(The Twelve Chakra System, at the time of this writing, is a completely new system, introduced specifically for these books and the advanced information contained therein..). My first book is Handbook for Cosmic Consciousness. ISBN-13:978-1086826852, Aug. 16, 2019). Some of which are quoted in later chapters.

When we tire of playing with lower vibrations, equivalent to doing endless scales on the piano, we discover simultaneous expansion/contraction. This concept brings a whole alternative universe into view. It means finally getting off the wheel and expanding out into the universe...

MANIFESTATION OF CONSCIOUSNESS

Consciousness is one of the greatest mysteries we have. We know we have it, but what exactly is it? There is a consistent pattern in all manifestations. This includes all life forms, from the simplest microorganisms to the most advanced humans among us. *They all exhibit some kind of consciousness, as do all the lower kingdoms: grass, trees, and even the Earth itself.*

FIRST, we have the naturally developing life on our planet. Results that represent billions of years of trial and error through planetary intelligence.

SECOND, we have a spiritual component that tries to influence the first. Sometimes successfully and sometimes not. Some scholars insist that this spiritual component came first. Others believe that nature came first. *However, the two disparate forces are a single force created simultaneously with a unified purpose. Each reflection of the other.*

THIRD, what is your part in all of this? Why are you here in this rather uncomfortable situation? You know deep down that you are spiritually immortal and that something went to a lot of trouble to get you here.

Basic Structure

All creation is based upon differences in vibration. Consciousness takes advantage of this as it manipulates its many viewpoints or configurations. The physical component contains the lower vibrations, while the spiritual component contains the higher. Because there is a constant struggle for unification, much like keys on a piano, neither the higher nor the lower vibrations are superior.

Inside Versus Outside

Diametrically opposed, half of the world exists spiritually on the inside (figuratively speaking),, while the other half exists on the outside. Each is content with their beliefs, sure that they are the entitled ones. Those on the outside believe they are free from the vanity and pettiness of the inside, confident that they have a ticket to the penthouse.

The inside is mostly unaware of what is outside, believing that only they are penthouse-bound. The sad fact is that both inside and outside are entitled but in separate ways. The reason for this is that there is only one consciousness divided into many parts.

Regardless of where you are in your expansion of consciousness, you will encounter the need to balance your viewpoint with its opposite by incorporating it. Otherwise, you may find that you are stalled in your spiritual progress. All souls take many incarnations to realize this simple fact. Balance includes up with down, right with left, forward with backward, expansion with contraction, love with hate, emotions with intellect, physical with spiritual, future with past, etc... Balance, balance, balance...

One Note Versus Cords

If you have ever watched a child attempt to play the piano, you realize a child usually plays one note at a time.

Whereas the accomplished pianist plays multiple notes in the most wonderful way.

Spiritually we are the same way. Some of us use the same couple of notes one at a time. Others are spiritual virtuosos, having mastered spiritual chords.

Emotional Balance

Story...Paul

I looked at Paul; he was one of those fun, roly-poly type of guys who you could never guess his age. I said, "Emotional balance is remarkably like a teeter-totter. Remember when you were a kid on the playground? You would get on one side, and your partner would climb on the other. Whoever was closest to the ground would push off. One of you was always up while the other was down.

Using this example, emotional imbalances resemble a teeter-totter. If you are up, you are soon down with no idea how you got there.

The trick is to level the teeter-totter so it is neither up nor down but perfectly level. Emotional balance, in the same way, needs to be flat, being neither for nor against, this opens up new and completely different avenues of emotional and spiritual exploration."

"Wait a minute," Paul said. "How in the world is something like this accomplished?"

I jumped in, "I know it sounds difficult, with so much emotion erupting in the world. It is almost as though we run on it. However, there are steps that can be taken that are proven to work."

Paul flicked his overly large ears, "I am all ears."

I continued, "A good place to start is to emotionally detach from your position. Human emotions are always limitations. For example, back to the piano analogy, individual notes are raw emotions, whereas a chord might represent love or compassion.

Even love has a dual nature. There are two kinds of basic love. The first is non-personal love, where you unconditionally love everyone and everything." The second is personal possessive love where you claim ownership of the object you love. My wife, my husband, my house, my car, etc.

However, there is a third and more complete kind of love. It is the perfect combination of possessive and non-possessive love. It is the golden completeness of Universal love, which manifested first, and subdivided into its two components. (We will discuss, in Part Two, how to achieve this wonderful state...."

Emotional Detachment

On a roll, I continued. "Base emotions, emotional outbursts, tantrums, hitting inanimate or animate objects, etc., are sure signs that a person is spiritually stunted. Immature behavior is learned and has become habitual. To advance spiritually, it is essential to transcend all forms of anger, avoiding even a momentary lapse, as though it were as bad as shopping at your market naked. This, of course, takes constant awareness to root out.

Emotional detachment from one's position means first taking stock of what your position is. It could be fervent political or religious positions. It could be as simple as becoming too vocal about your favorite sports team or as dire as secretly wanting to murder your awful neighbor. *You are one-sided to the exclusion of the other side.* This leads to spiritual imbalance." End

Story…Socks

I used to have a pair of grey socks. I always wanted the socks to be right-side-out. (I was a bit superstitious at the time). The problem was that I had trouble telling if they were or not… If they were correct, I could tell right away. However, if they were wrong-side-out, I couldn't be sure. However, if one was right side out, and the other was wrong, I could tell right away. And so it is with universal truths versus false truths.

Truth is obvious, while false truth is not…please remember, when something is true, it will have a solid feeling, or it will shine out with a particular light or ring with a certain clarity of sound, it will feel good. If it is not true, or only partially true, that solidness, light, sound, or feeling will be missing or subdued. When in doubt, it is most likely false. Intuition is a sure way to tell if it is true or not. Trust your feelings…

Our senses have become dulled after a lifetime bombardment of half-truths and false-trues…

Story…Paul-2

My friend Paul and I were continuing our discussion of metaphysical truisms.

I claimed that good and evil were different sides of the same coin. Paul had a tough time understanding what was meant by this.

I explained. "Good and evil are neither good nor evil. They are merely two halves of the same truth. Universal Good, for example, combines false good with evil. Evil is not even a concept until Universal Good is broken apart into its two constituent parts.

In fact, evil is created and brought into being by false-good... They are two halves of one thing, which is Universal Good.' I emphasized. 'It's one of the most misunderstood truths we have!"

Paul was confused. "What good does knowing this do me?"

I explained. "Universal Good has no opposite. It allows you to move through life without running into negative obstacles of self-created misery."

"Suppose I believe you." Paul countered. "How could I ever attain such a level?"

"I know it sounds difficult," I began. "It takes constant self-awareness to break old, rooted habits. It will take time and effort, but eventually, it will change your life." I paused for effect. "Understand that you are most likely in a position of good versus evil. This position has spawned such sayings as "No good deed goes unpunished." or "Waiting for the other shoe to drop."

Paul laughed. "I never knew there was anything wrong with that. I just thought that was how life worked."

I jumped in. "You and everyone else. Out of balance positive. How many books and movies try to teach us about that very thing? Extremely poor to extraordinarily rich and back again. I'm on top of the world one day and begging for change the next."

"OK," Paul said, beginning to understand. "I always thought it was just bad luck or karma."

"Unfortunately, that's what most people believe. The trick is to accept and incorporate the opposite."

I thought for a moment. "A good example is good with evil."

Paul looked puzzled. "You mean that I have to become evil?"

"Of course not." I laughed. "By blending the two, evil disappears, and what's left is Universal Good. Understanding that false good is not the truth but is instead dangerous and misleading. (Jesus gave his life trying to teach us this hard-to-understand fact..).

Understanding this simple concept is one of the most important steps you can take now, at your level of spiritual development, on the road to Superconsciousness." End

Summary

Universal good, which manifested first, is the combination of its components, false good and evil. These components are two sides of a single coin. You can call these opposing forces false good and evil. *The amazing fact is that false good **creates** evil... Out of balance positive, manifesting its twin.* Just to reiterate, out of balance, good (false good) creates an undesirable opposing result (evil). Jesus and his evil brother, Lucifer, are good examples of this difficult-to-understand conundrum…

PART TWO
Exercises

Take your time, and read slowly, carefully doing the exercises. Being in a hurry will only slow down your progress…slow is fast…Make sure you are comfortable with each exercise before going on. You can always come back and repeat an exercise if need be… You have the rest of your life, and beyond, to master this...

Your physical perceptions are confined to your five senses. Some of us, especially women, have developed a sixth sense, which we call intuition. Your sense of sight allows you to see into the third dimension. Your sense of hearing, smell, taste, and touch all allow you to perceive different vibratory levels in the third dimension. Note that none of these senses give you access to any place other than the 3D. As you develop your sense of intuition, you begin to sense there may be other dimensions, other than just the third dimension, in which you seem to live.

We see that the 3D, from your viewpoint, is outward facing and that the 4D is a mirror image universe of the 3D that, as a viewpoint, is inward facing. (A perfect example of this is a man, third dimensional, and a woman, fourth dimensional). We also find we cannot, as a unified viewpoint, easily experience both dimensions at the same time, something that needs to be mastered if we wish to progress. The techniques that follow are designed to solve this monumental problem.

It has been stated that the fifth configuration, or viewpoint (or fifth dimension), is composed of its two halves, the third and fourth dimensions combined. You will now learn how to, through these techniques, develop this combined viewpoint.

Remember that when you descended into the plane of duality, you had to divide into a half person, split between male and female…

There are several steps involved. We will go slowly through them.

I believe we can assume that you are still stuck in the 3D. You may think you are not. This is part of the power of 3D illusion. Before you can take the first step, on the road to fifth configurational proficiency, you need to be willing to let go on some level, of all that you are and all that you know.

Your ego will fight hard to convince you that what is being said here is all nonsense and a waste of time. You cannot really blame it for not wanting to be dethroned.

Your ego can be like a wanton child. It cares not about adult concerns and wants only what it thinks it wants when it wants it. It is, however, necessary in the continuum of existence of everyone, to mature to a point where the ego is willing to forego some of its immediate pleasures in favor of continuing evolutionary development.

What you will accomplish in the first step is as follows: A shift from the third configurational or dimensional viewpoint to the fifth configurational viewpoint. This means going from the familiar forward progression of time and events to a combination of inward and outward at the same time. (WHAT???)

It was mentioned that in order to progress, it is necessary to give up everything you are and everything you know. However, this does not mean jumping off of the bridge in a Ureka moment. This transition must be slow and easy. Let your higher power guide you in this fundamental stage...If you are not sure how to do this, look to your intuition and perhaps prayer if you are so inclined...

Meditation Techniques
Beginning Levels

Exercise One

• An especially critical point to be aware of is that acquiring the Fifth configuration also means EXPANDING IN SIZE in terms of your internal viewpoint and consciousness. You are about the size of a ping-pong ball or smaller. This means you can only experience a single chakra at a time as you travel within your being. Without a degree of mastery (such as possessed by dedicated monks), it is difficult, if not impossible, to travel at will from one center to the next. In the completed fifth-dimensional viewpoint, you will have expanded to a size larger than your physical body. This allows you to simultaneously experience all the previously separate centers, an extremely desirable spiritual position. (Note: this is entirely different than sensing your feet while sensing your hands...etc.).

• There is a physical center within your physical body that is the point where the third and fourth dimensions meet and pass through one another. It is the point in the center of the chest where you find an indentation. Its color is green. Within green, you are looking for the most central shade. In our meditation, it helps to have a physical location and a color to visualize. It is also associated with middle C for sound reference.

• There is a natural point of existence within you where you are balanced at your very center. This means you are conscious of the outside from the very center of your being. This place is the physical place at the center of the chest. (Heart Chakra)

• This meditation technique is to help you identify where the starting point is. If you can identify with your heart center at the sternum and green, this should help you find the correct placement.

• This portion of the exercise will be devoted to the beginning level of Meditation Techniques. You will start by concentrating on "opening" and warming up the "Heart center" located in the middle of the chest at the sternum, and not the actual area where the physical heart is located. (Feel for the indentation located between the breasts or pectoral muscles). You need to learn and practice these techniques frequently to prepare you for the more advanced Configurational Meditations, which are necessary to progress. (Becoming proficient should not take more than fifteen minutes a day).

• A centering process needs to take place to bring you into the heart center. This can be accomplished through stimulation of the heart center by rubbing it in a circular motion with the fingertips of one of your hands. (I use a counterclockwise motion, but you might find clockwise better for you). Do this until you can feel some heat begin to generate there. It might also help to visualize an opening middle to light green flower. (With practice, this center can feel quite warm, if not hot. If you do not feel warmth right away, this is OK. It will come with time).

Exercise Two

The differences in configurations are how you perceive them. Remember,

you are looking at something that is <u>*complete from an incomplete viewpoint.*</u> As your viewpoint improves, you will experience more complete configurations.

As you progress in your meditation, you need to heal up some of the third and fourth configurational damage that has accumulated at the various centers (chakras).

We always begin our meditation at the heart center because it centers us and allows a balanced expansion. *The heart center in most people is full of pain and disappointments.* It is the center of relationships. It is through this center that you share your love with others.

When you experience pain through broken relationships or the death of pets or loved ones, this center tends to shut down rather than go through the natural grieving process that keeps the heart center healthy. When this center shuts down it locks away the pain as though in a feel-proof vault, by freezing time. The result is that this person is no longer able to love or participate fully in any relationship.

The reason people allow this center to shut down is for the obvious reason of not wanting to feel the pain. There is an inordinate fear of opening this center and having to unfreeze those moments that have been waiting all this time to be felt. The pain felt there is never as bad as it was thought to be and usually dissipates in a matter of seconds. Sometimes, there is grieving, but it only lasts a brief time, soon to be replaced by the joy of being able to feel love again.

Healing The Heart-Center

It is human nature to avoid pain, so we quickly stuff it in our heart center, where we forget about it. We know the pain is still there but are afraid to take it out, not wanting to feel it. Some of this pain might be many years old, still waiting to be faced while diminishing our ability to love. We will now spend some time on healing the heart center…

Warming The Heart-Center

Also, notice if your heart center feels cold. If so, repeat the exercise until it feels warm. The cold is felt as an icy feeling on the palm of your hand, indicating that this center is shut down! Rub the center in a circular motion until warmth is felt. Or simply lay your dominant hand flat on this center until you feel some warmth replacing the cold…

You will start by concentrating on opening and warming up the heart center in the middle of the chest at the sternum, not the actual area where the physical heart is located. (Feel for the indentation between the breasts/pecs). Rubbing your heart center helps to warm it up. You need to practice these beginning techniques daily to prepare you for the more advanced techniques. (It should not take over five or ten minutes a day to become proficient. It is important to include it in your daily routine.

Pain In The Heart-Center

During this process, you might feel pain in your heart center. These are shards of energy. They range from black to clear. All shards can be removed either by yourself or by a sensitive friend.

Removing Energy Shards

Each shard contains an encapsulated memory of a painful experience. To remove them, locate a particular pain and feel for the shard. It exists on the lower etheric plane rather than physically. Once a shard is located, take hold of it with your fingertips and pull it out.

This is done more with your imagination than with your physical sense. You can identify the cause of that shard as you extricate it. The grieving process is fast. Not as bad as you feared it would be. Many times, over in a matter of seconds.

Story…Feeling Dead

I was doing some energy work on a friend. She said, "I feel dead. I can't even feel love for my children."

I looked at her. "I know exactly how you feel. Before I cleared my heart center, I couldn't feel anything except negative emotions."

She instantly perked up. "Clearing the heart center. Is this something you can do?"

I tried not to smile. I was hoping she would ask that very question. "I could try," I said and began to explain the process. "Your heart center is located at the indentation between your breasts and not at the actual heart center."

I could see that she was a little nervous. "There is nothing to be nervous about. I don't need to touch you, and no need to disrobe." I continued to explain the procedure. "Your heart center is the center where you feel all the good stuff like love and joy. All the things that make life worth living."

I pointed to her heart center. "All the pain of life gets stuffed in there." The reason is simple. You don't like to feel pain, so you freeze it in time within this center."

I continued, "What I will do is feel for shards of energy embedded there. I will tug on each one I find and ask you what that was. After you tell me, I will ask for your permission to remove it."

"Ok," she nodded. "Do whatever it takes."

I am an empath. This has both its good points and bad. This was one of the good ones: my ability to feel another's pain for the purpose of healing. I placed the fingers of my right hand about an inch above her heart center at the sternum. Right away, I could feel many shards—no wonder she couldn't feel anything. I tugged on one of the larger ones. "Can you feel that?"

She began to panic. "No! Not that one! It is too painful. It is my dead son."

"Sorry," I said. "Let's move on to a different one." I felt for a smaller shard. Finding one, I tugged on it. "What about this one?"

'Yes," she said, noticeably relieved. "That is from all the way back in high school." She laughed. "I had completely forgotten about it. My boyfriend dumped me for another girl. I was devastated."

"Ok to pull this one out?"

"Yes, please. I can't believe that it is still there after all these years."

As I concentrated, I was able to visualize getting hold of it between my thumb and forefinger. It came right out. I visualized it disappearing as I flung it towards the floor.

She had a look of astonishment. "You really did it. I actually felt that," she laughed, getting more excited. "Please do another one."

I carefully picked over the shards (they felt prickly to my fingers), pulling them out one at a time in order of size. Several of them caused her to weep a bit, such as her dog that she had to put to sleep. Finally, we were getting down to the last several shards. I knew about the one that was her son but not about the other two.

I pulled on the smaller of the three. "What is this one?"

"That was when my dad died." She began to tear up.

I suggested that we wait a day or two, giving her a chance to grieve a bit. She agreed.

It is best to be careful with the larger shards. Giving the person plenty of time to heal up. Usually, the grieving process lasts anywhere from a few seconds to several days. A week later, we were done. I had removed the last of the shards from her dead son.

She cried for about an hour, her head on my shoulder. She told me that she had been driving on the Freeway and looked down for only a moment, not noticing that traffic had stopped. "When I looked up, I was crashing into the car in front of me and my son, who had been sitting right next to me, was hurtling out of the front window. The first responders told me that they were having trouble finding his head. *They couldn't find his head!!!*" she began wailing and beating her fists on her thighs.

After a while, it subsided. A look of total relief washed over her face. She looked at me with such love in her eyes. "I can never repay you. You have saved my life and the happiness of my family. Please let me pay you."

I declined, thanking her, explaining that her gratitude was enough and that I never accepted payment because it interfered with my psychic abilities. I told her to think of it as one friend helping another.

How To Open Your Own Heart Center

Open your heart center by concentrating on the fingers of your right hand and pointing them into the area of the sternum at the center of your chest. Make an opening motion by slowly widening your fingers. As this center opens, you may feel warmth begin to radiate out from it. Visualize a green flower opening…

Typically, expect to feel something wedged into the center of your heart center (this is not the physical heart) It is like frozen energy that varies in size from a thick hair to a toothpick. It is usually clear in color.

•Next, with your dominant hand, feel for a bed of shards that feel like a miniature cactus. Concentrate on a particular shard. Take a hold of the tip of it with your fingertips and gently pull it out.

This takes place in the lower etheric plane and not in the actual physical. While watching the procedure, other clairvoyants described what the object looked like as I pulled it out, which usually matched my earlier description.

I would dispose of the frozen energy by flinging it down towards the ground.

•Continue to pull shards from your heart center until you can feel no more shards. Give yourself adequate time to recover from any grieving you might experience...

To go to the next level of meditation, you need to clear your heart center. You can do this by using the procedures above. I would suggest stimulating your heart center every day. I have literally worn holes in a couple of my t-shirts doing this.

If you cannot feel any shards, do not worry about it. Just go on to the next exercise. (You most likely have a friend or two who are a bit psychic. If they are empathic or sensitive, read the technique written above to them and ask them if they would be willing to help you. It might be fun to start a workshop for heart center clearing…Everyone could benefit from this!)

This concludes the exercise. Next time, we will examine in detail the techniques and results of opening the throat and top of the Solar Plexus centers.

S Solar Plexus

The exercises below are for advanced students. If you have trouble doing them or feel that they are too hard, or that you are not benefiting from them, then I recommend forming a workshop with a friend or a group of like-minded friends… (This is a good idea even if you are having great success…and fun as well…)

In the last Exercise, you examined some techniques for opening and clearing the "Heart Center." In this exercise, you are going to learn how to open the "Throat Center" (all shades of blue) and "Upper Solar Plexus Center" (golden yellow), located just above the navel.

Notice that with each pair of centers we combine, the colors are complementary. (Opposites). This is another validation of this system.

The primary goal of your soul (as your Over-soul), is to come here to the third configuration from outside of linear time in order to help you manifest in full consciousness in accordance with the intent of the "Universal Mind." Along the way, you will discover simple remedial techniques that are not previously available and can be used by everyone immediately. Some of these techniques might easily overcome unapproachable human conditions. Information worth more than gold…

Expansion

I like using a balloon analogy because it nicely incorporates dual expansion without a lot of mental gymnastics…

You start with your balloon as a green bubble surrounding the heart center at your sternum. Visualize it as extending, perfectly round, out front and back, as well as top and bottom.

The "Throat Center" (blue) and "Top of the Solar Plexus Center" (golden yellow) are opposites. In a normally operating person, the Throat-Center is dominant. This produces a nice, blissful feeling of well-being in the solar plexus area. In people who are fearful, angry, or anxious, their Solar Plexus Centers have become dominant, which produces fear, anger, and anxiety. This is why people who suffer from this problem have difficulty speaking when they are afraid or angry. They become choked up with emotion. Reflux (stomach acid backing up to the throat) is a physical symptom of this condition. When they are angry, they find themselves saying things that they would never normally say, often causing irreparable damage to relationships with friends, co-workers, and loved ones. If this anger is channeled down to the lower centers, then physical violence might occur. (The pharmaceutical companies are getting rich in producing chemicals to mask this out-of-balance condition). The obvious remedy, then, is to re-establish the proper relationship between these two centers.

Exercise Four

(The hand positions mentioned below can be reversed, meaning, for example, where the right hand is indicated, substitute the left hand, and the same for the left hand, substitute the right hand. Try both methods and do whichever feels more comfortable). In the exercise below, you are asked to visualize various colors. It might be easier if you gathered the colors together before the meditation. You can use, for example, paper, crayons, ribbons, or fruit. The colors for this exercise are green, blue, dark yellow (male), or pink (female). Use whichever best suits you.

•Start the meditation by placing the fingers of your right hand together and pointing them in at your heart center at the center of your chest. (Your heart center is not found in the actual heart area. Instead, It is located at the indentation at the center of your chest at the sternum, between the breasts or pectorals).

Now, slowly open your fingers, visualizing a green flower opening.

•Next, place your left hand over the top of your solar plexus until you can feel some warmth there.

•Next, place your right hand at the throat center and gently tap it (located just below the Adam's apple), this is to wake it up.

•Next, make an opening gesture with the fingertips of your right hand at the throat center. As you slowly widen your fingers, feel the increased energy there. (Visualize your throat center as a blue flower opening. Continue to hold this center open as you start the next step).

•Next, with your left hand, make an opening gesture with your fingertips in at your upper solar plexus (just two inches above your navel); visualize your upper solar plexus as a dark yellow (most men) or pink (most women) flower opening. Your balloon should now have expanded from your throat center to the top of your solar plexus. (Understand that your consciousness is contained within the balloon. As your consciousness expands, begin to feel each involved center radiate warmth within your chest. Imagine that your mind is inside of the balloon, and you are happily looking out from within it. It is important to experience the balloon from inside of it. This might take some practice, but it must be mastered before you can continue..).

Your balloon, centered around the indentation at the center of your chest, is expanding from your Heart Center to your Throat Center and down to your Upper Solar Plexus Center. It will automatically absorb these colors, blue and dark yellow. At this point, it is important to visualize your balloon from the inside, as having expanded out, touching these indicated centers.

•You might want to continue this exercise until any feelings of fear, anger, or anxiety have subsided. If you have a lot of fear, anger, or anxiety, you might want to repeat the meditation whenever you can throughout the day until the feelings subside and are replaced by feelings of well-being.

I cannot stress how important these exercises are. They are not only life-changing but will also help place you on the right path for the rapid advancement of your spiritual evolution. I have declined to charge thousands of dollars for this course because it is priceless and has nothing to equal it, existing in this time frame, and as such, should never be reduced to a monetary value for fear of losing sight of its importance...You have worked long and hard to reach this point. You deserve to have it. Most people will not appreciate this work simply because they are not advanced enough to understand it...I made it available in the hopes that there might be a few, like you, who would be ready. (I was advised not to make such a work available in this time period, except as a precursor for advanced students existing in the future. I disregarded that advice, and now, I am glad I did because of you).

I cannot begin to tell you how much I appreciate you...

This meditation works. You might want to share it with your friends as a workshop…

- This may sound silly, but it helps to talk to your solar plexus. This is where your "inner child" lives. If you have chronic anxiety, then this would be a good technique to cultivate. While rubbing your upper solar plexus, say something like this: "I am here now, and everything is alright. You don't have to worry; I am in charge now, and I will take care of everything." Feel that part of you relaxing in trust. Another variation of this is to pat your solar plexus and say over and over, "You are a good boy (girl). I am here now, and everything is alright." This should reduce the level of anxiety or fear.
- This concludes the Exercise. Next time, you will examine in detail the techniques and results of opening the Mouth and Bottom of the Solar Plexus centers.

Opening Mouth To Bottom Of Solar Plexus

The colored objects needed for this exercise are indigo (a very dark blue), and bright yellow.

The Mouth Center (indigo), represents abstract power (hidden or behind the scenes), and spirituality. Its counterpart, located at the lower solar plexus (Bright yellow), is raw courage and abstract intellect (general rather than specific). Courage, without a sense of spirituality, can degenerate into foolhardy sexual antics, destructive behavior, and even rage, and therefore, spirituality must lead. Spirituality without the courage to act leads to physical inaction.

To balance these two centers, you need to expand your balloon at the heart center, from the mouth to the lower solar plexus.

A WAY OUTSIDE THE BOX

In the following series of events, the procedure is as easy as riding on a conveyor belt. Meaning that you have little to remember or accomplish once started.

You start at the Heart Center because it is the vibrational middle of the color spectrum (green). It is then a simple matter of moving one level at a time away from the center (both up and down the color scale), which results in matching, for example, the first set of opposite pairs (blue and golden yellow). Using a balloon as a conveyance, this endeavor will become automatic.

Visualize your balloon, centered around your sternum, as expanding to your mouth center (indigo), and to your Lower Solar Plexus (bright yellow), located below the navel. See the balloon naturally absorbing these colors. Your consciousness is comfortably inside of it, and you are looking out from within it.

Feel a pleasant change in your consciousness as your balloon expands within you. You actually feel yourself expanding in size…Visualize yourself as inside the balloon, expanding. Become the balloon…

(See diagram below)

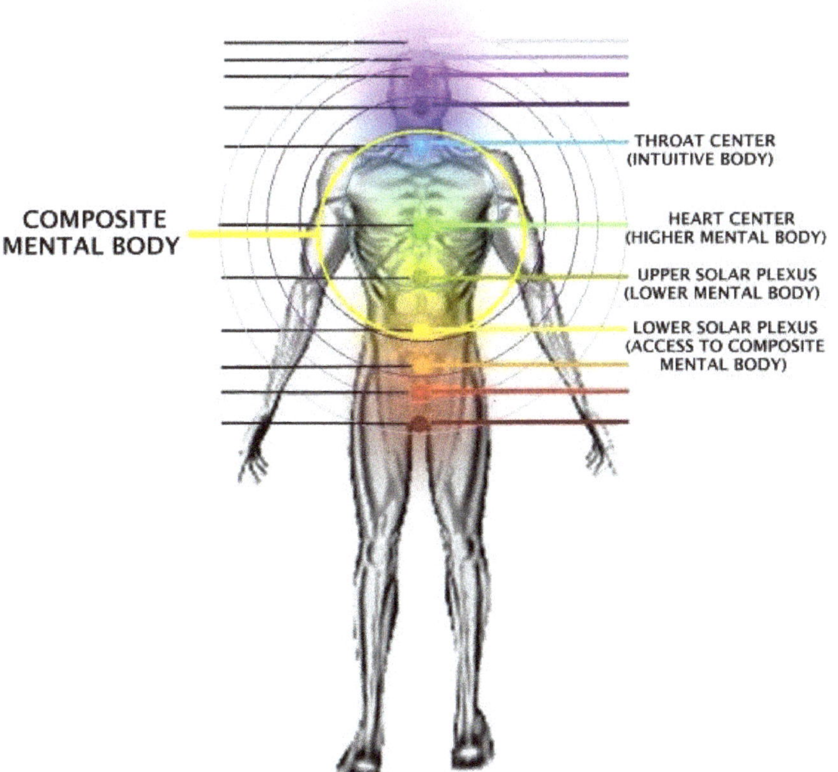

Diag. Mental Bodies

Exercise Five
Between The Eyes And Splenic Center

The colored objects needed for this exercise are purple and orange.

The centers you will open in this Exercise are the "Between the Eyes Center," also called the "Third Eye," (located between the eyes), and the "Splenic Center," (called this because of its association with the spleen), located between the lower Solar Plexus and the Sexual Center. The color of the Between the Eyes Center is purple. It is the center of willpower and concentration. People who use this center are noted for their tenacity and focus.

The color of the Splenic Center is orange. It is the center that produces your physical life force. This center is responsible for physical vitality. The vital orange energy gives a person a zest for life and a desire to actively participate. The problems that occur when this center is not balanced by its counterpart (Third Eye, purple), can be manic in nature. By this, I mean a person will exhibit various levels of having to constantly do something. When left unchecked, it can result in nervous disorders, such as A.D.D and manic behavior.

When used by a balanced person, orange energy provides a nice, endless energy that is almost invisible. In other words, it is not hard on the nervous system while being wonderfully effective.

The Splenic center is located just above the sexual center and just below the lower solar plexus.

Next, tap the spot between your eyes to wake it up. Do this with your eyes closed. Once you have done this, gently massage the orange center until you feel both centers blend in, and extend your balloon from the third eye to just above the Sexual center.

Visualize your balloon and consciousness as having expanded from your Third Eye Center, purple, located just above your nose, to your Splenic Center, orange, located just above the Sexual Center. Your balloon, which is now quite large, has automatically absorbed these additional colors.

I like using the balloon analogy because it incorporates the expansion/contraction idea and easily moves us into the proper positions without a lot of mental contortions…

This concludes the Exercise. Next time, you will examine in detail the techniques and results of opening the Crown and Pelvic centers.

Exercise Six
Pairing The Crown And Pubic Centers

The colored objects needed for this exercise are Violet and Burgundy.

A WAY OUTSIDE THE BOX

In this exercise you will examine a technique for achieving the addition of the paired Crown and Pubic centers to your growing list.

The "Crown" center is known as the thousand-petaled lotus. It encircles the head like a band crossing the forehead area. Access to this center opens tremendous levels of clairvoyant knowledge, power, and abilities, not the least of which is the transmutation of female sexual energy into a creative force. (Kundalini)

The sexual center ("Pubic" center) is renowned for its potential problems if left to its own devices.

Your expanding balloon, which represents your expanding viewpoint and consciousness, has grown quite large.

This time, you will expand your balloon from the Crown Center, Violet, to the Sexual Center, burgundy.

Before you begin this exercise, repeat the previous exercises starting at the Heart Center, up to and including the paired centers, Third Eye to the Orange Center just above the sexual center…this is important!

Next, with your eyes closed, place the palm of your right hand on your forehead. Next, place your left hand over your Sexual Center. Once you have done this, feel the counterbalancing force of the sexual center begins to vibrate. Rather than feeling sexual, it should blend in with the other centers in the form of radiant power and good feelings. If you are not feeling anything, make sure that you are spending enough time opening each center, (see previous meditations), especially that your heart center is as warm as you can make it. (A circular or light scratching motion at the small indentation at the center of your chest will help warm this center up).

Your balloon is now expanded from your head to your Sexual Center.

This concludes the Exercise. Next time, you will examine in detail the techniques and results of opening the Top of the Head Center and Coccyx Center.

Exercise Seven

This is the last in the series of Fifth Configurational Meditations. The exercise after this one will take you into the pure sixth dimension or configuration of the void. You will have expanded your balloon consciousness to encompass your body completely. *Remember that you started as the size of a ping pong ball.*

Top Of The Head Center To The Coccyx Center

Repeat the meditations starting with the Heart Center and expanding your balloon until it resides at the Crown and down to the Sexual Center.

Next, find a spot at the very top and center of your head. By massaging this spot, you will activate the center. The Prudent body is responsible for controlling the spiritual energy flow through all eleven bodies.

When working properly with the other ten, this body becomes what is called a conscience. It is counterbalanced (as its opposite), with the physical (meat) body whose center is called the Coccyx or Coccyx center, located as where the name might indicate. The reason we each have only eleven chakras instead of twelve is that the sexual center comprises two separate centers. Red-Aries for a man (Aries resides outside of the Christ or Creative plane, whose complement is green) and Burgundy-Virgo for a woman. (Later in our hunt for the elusive first dimension, Aries, we will discover a second reason).

You have seen each pair of polarized bodies as you have progressed through the meditation, but this polarity of the Prudent and Physical bodies is particularly unique in that both bodies interface with the void. The physical body interfaces with the outside 3D world. It is a physical boundary that keeps you from spilling out into space. The prudent body also interfaces with space, but it is with "inside" space that is found to reside outside of your eleven bodies as "inner space," a place separate from, but occupying the same space as your physical form (more on this later).

As ,"mentioned before, it can be activated by massaging the "top of the head center." There is a high-pitched whistle associated with this center. You may or may not "hear" this whistle (about 12 KHz). You may also feel a localized pressure or energy at the spot at the top of your head. Pisces often hear this whistle...

Once you feel that you have sufficiently stimulated this center, become aware of the Coccyx center by placing your hand over it from the back. This will sensitize your physical body. The net result you are looking for is to expand your balloon, to completely engulf all eleven bodies, extending from the innermost and highest vibrational body (ultraviolet), to the outermost and lowest vibrational body, the physical body (dark red).

This is the completed Fifth configuration. Please do not look for anything spectacular to happen at this point. You may or may not feel any different. This does not matter. There is, currently, nothing you want to use here.

This concludes the Exercise.

Prelude To Sixth Dimensional Techniques

Theory

Your consciousness is divided into two basic parts, higher and lower, consciousness or vibrations. The lower consciousness is what you are most familiar with. This includes all that you experience as reality on a daily basis. However, there is a hidden part, the higher, that is outside of your normal experience. It exists in the void just outside of your conscious range. This part is called Cosmic Consciousness, a necessary addition to your consciousness because it allows you to expand beyond the three-dimensional confines within which you find yourself.

More than any other step you can take, at this juncture, acquiring Cosmic Consciousness is the most important one for you now. (Note: I am not talking about the Etheric planes, nor the Astral planes. In fact, none of the readily known planes of existence. I am talking about the void of the sixth dimension, which exists completely outside of the plane of creation, a viewpoint constructed of an aggregate of six separate levels of stacked vibration, or six dimensions or configurations).

As you work through this exercise, it is important to visualize your heart center (located at the center of your chest) expanding. Feel your heart center encompassing each pair of centers as you progress through the steps.

I grew up with the seven-chakra system and never questioned it until it no longer met the need to expand my understanding of this kind of unique knowledge. I struggled with the Twelve-Chakra system, trying to comprehend the immenseness of this ancient labyrinthine knowledge.

It took me years to put it all together, and to my delight, I beheld a hidden jewel crafted by spiritual giants long gone.

Every piece, like a gigantic puzzle, had to be present and fit precisely with all of the other pieces. I began to see the beauty of how perfectly blended and synergistic everything was.

I spent every waking moment immersed in its demand for exactness. Each piece would unfold three more pieces in a seemingly endless flood of epiphanies.

Reminder

Remember to allow your expanding heart center to merge and blend with each opposing pair. This is actually the easiest part because once started, it is automatic. You are just along for the ride. By using the balloon, it gives you a tangible to visualize and feel. Inside of the balloon is your expanding consciousness. Every step you have taken has actually expanded you.

A large part of what you are accomplishing is through imagination and visualization. Believe it, and it will happen.

Visualize your expanding ball of consciousness encountering the lowest center and touching the highest. You are inside of it.

Take your time with this exercise. The expansion/contraction is a natural motion that constantly moves in its predestined path. Once you start riding, it will automatically take you to your next predestined destination.

Fear is the only thing that can stop or slow it down (your perception of it). In addition to assisting with the acquisition of successive centers, your focus is not clinging to each center as you progress. Letting go of emotional constraints, especially fear, is the most important part of this exercise.

Understand that the only thing that is changing is your expanding viewpoint. You started at your heart center, and now it has expanded to encompass your entire body. The subsequent motion will project you outside your body into the void of the Cosmic Principle, where your viewpoint will continue expanding. You are much safer in the cosmic void than in your everyday existence in the Fifth Configuration. I spend a lot of my free time there…

Let's take walking as an example of letting go. Each step is an act of falling, saved by the next step. One must let go of the previous step and accumulate the next one to walk. We are spiritual toddlers learning how to walk.

Transition From Fifth To Sixth Config

At this point, refresh your previous meditation; you will have expanded from the top of your head to the bottom of your torso. Now, all you must do is wait. You are safer here than in your bed. (Remember that you have traveled from center to center, in opposite directions as you expanded/contracted).

Once the above steps are achieved, the next step will be automatic. Your consciousness will emerge into the void. Be prepared for this next step because, at first, you will see only blackness. It is important to maintain this position because you are moving faster than the speed of light toward the outer barrier that encapsulates your universe. Even at this speed, it takes time to accomplish.

It is extremely important to master this relatively easy step. Not doing so will keep you from accessing the next series of abilities. Remember, there is no rush. Understand that you have already accomplished this in the future. All you must do is catch up with yourself through practice, much like the amazing violin virtuoso who was awful when first starting.

Understand that you are an expanding ball of consciousness. (We are used to thinking of ourselves as a physical body with a forward viewpoint. You are no longer focused on your physical body. You are now in something I am calling an expanding Stellar body).

Bright Star

You will know you have arrived when you see a bright star in front of you. (This star is the Universal Sun, composed of all the stars and galaxies in your universe).

The Sixth Configuration

Once you leave the confines of the 5th config, you automatically enter the void of the 6th config. (You have left the confines of your everyday universe and have now achieved the Cosmic Configuration or Cosmic Consciousness).

In the void, you are facing in an outward direction. Since there is nothing here but void, you see only blackness, which surrounds and protects your tiny universe. (Let me stress that unlike the 3D there is absolutely nothing here in the void that can harm you. It is one of my favorite places, and I spend a lot of time here meditating).

You are moving out as an expanding ball of consciousness at a rate of speed much faster than the speed of light. It is important to maintain your position with patience. In approximately one to three minutes or more, you will have expanded out to the size of your entire universe, where you will bounce off a barrier. This impenetrable barrier is the shell that holds your universe, much like an eggshell contains an egg.

(It is essential to maintain during this period. Although you are traveling faster than the speed of light, it still takes time to traverse your entire universe.

I was confused by this period of blackness when I first experienced it. Thinking that I had dead-ended, I would quit and lose what I had gained, winding up back in my body extremely disappointed in my lack of progress. I did this more times than I care to say…

Finally, with nothing left to lose and not knowing what to expect, I decided to remain in the blackness until something happened, even if it took hours.

I was so happy when I finally bounced off the barrier after a few minutes, which reversed the direction of my expanding ball of consciousness to that of a contracting one, and I beheld the beautiful white light of the star before me!)

Mechanics Explained

The actual mechanics of what happened to you upon observing the white star are these: you, (as an expanding ball of energy) bounced off the barrier and automatically reversed your direction.

The star you see in front of you is the universe you were in before you started. It was the fifth configuration (5th dimension), but now, viewed from the void of the sixth configuration (6th dimension), it has become the seventh configuration (7th dimension). I know this is a lot to digest and may seem a bit hale and hearty, but I assure you that as you progress, it will become clearer.

The reason the configurations are so numbered is because of the order in which we encountered them.

Fifth Configuration

The 5th config. is *everything inside of creation,* existing as the *Creative Principle.* The 5th config resolves into a single Universal Star (7th config). when viewed from the outside void or *Cosmic Principle.* Just like a building—rooms, offices etc., on the inside. A monolithic structure when viewed from the outside.

Seventh Configuration

Once you contact the barrier, there is a reversal of direction. Once you have reversed, you will see the solitary star (Universal star). This star is all of the creation in your universe. This lone star is now the seventh configuration (dimension). Your viewpoint has changed from the labyrinthian fifth (inside of creation) to the pure simplicity of the seventh (outside of creation).

As you continue to move toward the ball of white light (this phase is automatic), it will take you to the seventh configuration, a world of silver-white light and bliss—a world of crystalline delight.

However, just as you feel you have arrived in Nirvana, you will suddenly find yourself, once again, traversing space in complete blackness. And just as you had maintained previously, know that you are traveling back to the barrier. Just let it happen. Eventually you will again bounce off the outer barrier and see the solitary star once again.

Unless you enjoy bouncing around, you will now find it necessary to discover the eighth configuration.

Eighth Configuration

Your bouncing consciousness is now responding to the eighth configuration in synchronization with your heartbeat and your expanded heart center (still based at the sternum).

The heartbeat of the eighth configuration expands out to the confines of the sphere that contains your universe and then bounces off, reversing its direction. It continues to collapse until it bounces off your Heart Center at the sternum, where it begins its expansion over again. In order to transcend the eighth configuration, it is necessary to let go of the heartbeat and allow it to continue beating, just as you do with your regular heartbeat. Once you let go, you will experience a gentle balancing sensation. Let the heartbeat continue without holding on…this configuration has been doing this since before you were born…

VISUALIZATION

Visualize yourself as a ball, expanding and then contracting. Now, slowly visualize the expansion and contracting taking place within you. Stay above it, like your physical heartbeats without your supervision.

Visualize your heart center located at the indentation between the pectoral muscles/breasts, expanding out to the limits of the sphere of your universe and back again. Since the expansion/contraction is instantaneous, it happens within the time of your regular heartbeat. Just visualize it as a natural part of your being. No need to interfere or control it. It has been doing this continuously since you were in your mother's womb.

As you master the universal heartbeat, you are opening the golden love contained in this center. It starts as a pleasant, warm glow in your chest area. It slowly expands to include your face and hands. It is easily seen by those close to you as a golden halo…

Summary

The Golden configuration is your Universal Heart (golden light), and its vibration is one of universal love or Christ Consciousness. Whereas, the seventh configuration is the silver light of consummate compassion and bliss, Krishna Consciousness, which is the quality of your Universal heart. Universal love is bliss in motion or magnetic expansion that impinges upon others.

Remember everything that is happening originates from your heart-center at your sternum and your heartbeat... Like a series of lenses or layers, you have compounded the quality of your heart center as it expands out to the eighth configuration. As your viewpoint changes, it begins to profoundly affect your level of beingness. Everything you are experiencing was there before you activated it…just waiting for you to evolve to this level…

Just a word of caution…Christ Consciousness can become confusing, fraught with visions of grandeur, believing that you are Jesus returned… I fell into this trap, and it was uber-embarrassing!!! I was going around blessing everyone and scaring the hell out of my friends and relatives. Eventually, as I acquired the ninth configuration, I settled down…

Overwhelm

This is the real deal, and much easier than you might think).

It might be less intimidating for you to visualize the entire universe the size of a large crystal ball.

Remember, it is only your conscious viewpoint that is changing. Everything else remains the same.

It is interesting to realize that all the steps taken (from the first balancing of opposing centers to popping out into the void of the sixth configuration) are automatic, like a conveyor belt. Fear slows it down, but it can become quite an easy and exhilarating experience with practice.

Review

You exist in a series of cosmic puzzle boxes.

Not understanding these puzzles dooms you to wander around in the third dimension like a mindless zombie, indentured to work until you are too old to be of any use, and then you die, only to do it all over again...

However, it is possible to master 3D by solving these puzzles. This information, worth more than riches, is contained, step by step, here in this book. You have looked at quite a few of these puzzle boxes already. You will look at them again with a bit more detail a bit later…

Of course, I cannot do it for you. I can only point the way by sharing what has worked for me...please understand this may take some time. Like any endeavor worth mastering, time and effort must be expended. Unlike most of our endeavors, like becoming a good bowler or a decent chess player, this one can free you into an amazing reality, with the knowledge that you are in line with Universal Consciousness…And an unlimited future…(if I could do it, then so can you!)

Some technical information: when you were inside the white ball (star), where you were born and lived, your viewpoint was stuck in the confusing warren of the fifth configuration.

Once you exited the fifth configuration, you immediately entered the quiet void of the sixth configuration, where your fifth configurational viewpoint eventually became your seventh configurational viewpoint (moving from inside to outside, from Creative principle to Cosmic).

This is an extremely crucial point. The transition from the Creative Principle to the Cosmic is never clearer than now.

Viewed from the outside, all that you consider as creation is held inside the Creative Principle. Now viewing it from the outside, it is a solitary star. The only thing that has changed is your conscious viewpoint. Everything else is exactly as it was.

When your consciousness was trapped inside the fifth configuration, you did not know there was anything outside it, which is just the mind-numbing nature of the fifth configuration.

Technically, when you exited the fifth and were stationed outside of it, you could then view it from the sixth configurational Void as the seventh config (star).

This automatically places you in the eighth config, coordinated with your own heartbeat, which is its signature.

Notice that in the eighth, you are held in one-half of your total heartbeat, which moves outward and inward continually. This is key to finding the solution to transcending it.

If you find yourself bouncing back and forth in the 8d, it is because you are identifying your viewpoint with only one-half of your heartbeat.

Centered on your heart center, at your sternum, your expansion extends out to the entire inside surface of the universal barrier, where it reverses.

Next step, after you master riding above the eighth configuration simply return to your normal consciousness. Do this by letting go of the Cosmic principle and returning to your everyday viewpoint. This is automatic.

Knowing that you are in sync with the eight configurations, feel your heart expanding out to the confines of your universe and back again, the way it has been since you were born.

Once you have mastered this technique, you will have gained access to the ninth configuration.

The ninth is a power structure. It is a stable viewpoint rather than motion, allowing you to attract, in a third configuration, whatever you desire without opposition.

(All of your newfound attributes and powers are meant to be used in the third configuration. You are slowly accumulating the keys to 'Heaven on Earth.' For us, the earth is the focus of creation. Like a microscope, it takes all the lenses to see into the microcosm. A new kingdom is forming: the superhuman kingdom. Its formation is a natural progression in evolution. Be glad you are at the forefront of this gift to humankind.

Important Information

(Below is some extremely valuable information concerning your life experience and your absolute lack of responsibility for it. Pay close attention to this, for it will, if you accept it, change your basic understanding of life and your role in it. You may not like what is said, as it will cut across everything you have read and learned, and may even teach, about the subject, but it is, never-the-less, true).

Not Your Fault

As a struggling human being, bearing your daily slings and arrows (as a direct result of your soul's learning mistakes, when it manifested here as you), you are used to the madness of spending most of your time trying to turn chaos into order.

Most of us are completely unaware that we exist in the past. When your soul incarnated as you, it experienced your lifetime and then went on to the next incarnation as a completely different person, leaving you to continuously repeat your current lifetime, like a merry-go-around, until your soul returns as an Oversoul, when it will reeducate you, and help you to the next level of evolution. (In 3D, once something is in motion, forming a pattern, there is a strong tendency to repeat that pattern from then on).

Stored in the past, your lifetime is preserved indefinitely, immune to change or even the death of the universe.

It is only now that your Oversoul has returned that you are free of that repetition. As you extricate yourself from the never-ending cycle of your life, it will continue without you, like a constantly repeating movie, with the actors no longer taking part as sentient beings.

(It is common to believe we remember our past lives, believing that we, the personality, are incarnated into those lives. An effective way to get into a fistfight is to tell someone that this is their first and only incarnation. However, these memories are of something I call the Interim Soul. This is a remnant of your original soul, left behind to babysit you. It is this Interim Soul that has memories of past incarnations but not future ones).

I hate to break it to you, but as a personality (the Jerries, the Abrahams, or Sandras), this is your first and only incarnation. You are a product of your soul. Baby God/Goddess, as it were...the next step in evolution.

Don't worry; you play an extremely important part in the creation of evolving consciousness. Although you are a creation of your soul, your experience plays an indispensable, integral part in the puzzle that is the universal plan.

You are born into an untenable reality. Waking up on a tiny speck of dirt, spinning at two thousand miles per hour, revolving around a blazing star, in the middle of endless space, destined to die, along with everyone you care about. And then you learn that you came out of your mother???

Meanwhile, everyone is telling you that everything is all right, perfectly normal. "Stop asking such stupid questions, kid. Children are meant to be seen and not heard."

However, the good news is that you are the next generation in consciousness. You are far ahead of all consciousnesses that have not yet experienced the lower three-dimensional realities. Your future is unlimited.

How Do You Resolve Your Problem?

How do you correct your mistakes? Short answer: existing in the past you cannot! You did not cause any problems. You simply followed the script created by your soul when it was gathering experience here as you. We find ourselves, as individual personalities, repeating our scripts like long-running plays, trapped in the past 'Waiting for Godot.' However, you are responsible for your emotional growth!

Oversoul

Remember that your soul is an Angel learning through incarnation. When it realizes that it no longer needs to incarnate, it evolves to that of Oversoul.

The good news is that eventually, our respective souls reach a point where they no longer find it necessary to incarnate. It is then that your soul returns to you as an Oversoul tasked with re-educating you, freeing you from your endless repetition of reliving the same lifetime, endlessly reliving the same movie...

I believe that you, being here, reading this book, means that your Oversoul has returned to you, especially considering that you are still with me after reading all that I have slung at you. (Smiling…)

No One Left Behind

There is a purpose and a direction for each of us no matter how badly our lifetime has gone or how wonderfully. NO ONE is left behind. You are a unique pattern in a much larger puzzle. Every piece must fill its unique spot otherwise, the puzzle is incomplete.

Living a lifetime gets you into the game! Once started, you are in it forever, reaching out into ever-expanding consciousness and realization...This cannot happen unless you do the basics; much like the military, you must start at the bottom before you can rise in rank...It is essential for you to understand that although you seem to remember past lifetimes, these are not your memories!

If you have had a particularly wonderful lifetime, it may be difficult to let go of it. Letting go is a necessary step, allowing you to take instruction from your Oversoul and move on to the more advanced levels of existence. (Wasn't it Jesus who said, about the chances of a rich man entering heaven were as likely as passing through the eye of the needle..).

Resistance to letting go can not only impede your current progress, causing you to unnecessarily further repeat your lifetime but can simi-permanently lock you into it. Unfortunately, this dire repetition has seized most of your brothers and sisters who share your universe. I call this unenviable state "Divers Syndrome." It is a state of being where you, the Mind of your being, have so identified with your physical, three-dimensional body that you think that it is you... (I will spend some time comparing a Soul with a Mind a bit later).

Your current progress, indelibly written in the fabric of consciousness, ensures that your physical experience is locked into reality, forever repeating in a never-ending cycle, as a necessary anchor allowing you to expand out into infinity without fear of losing a foothold on physical reality. This repetition, which is automatic, goes on without the necessity of your being a conscious participant...allowing you to fly as free as a spiritual bird...without the need to worry about your physical being...

TIME TRAP A time trap is wanting to redo certain episodes that occurred in the past, perhaps something as simple as wanting to save someone or a pet from a premature death. Or as dire as escape going to prison.

Changing The Past

"Is it possible to change the past?"

The answer is yes, but the change is only temporary.

"Why is it temporary?"

The reason that the changes you make that are different from the original timeline are only temporary is because the desire to change something only lasts one iteration! This is primarily due to the original timeline always reverting back to its original status.

For example, let's say that in the original timeline, you experienced an easily avoidable car accident in which you were driving because of a momentary distraction that resulted in the killing of your family, had, in addition, resulted in an insatiable desire to change the outcome to one where the accident never occurred.

Although this desire doesn't change the current iteration, it does affect the next one. When you experience the next iteration, you will be able to avoid the tragic accident, thus saving your family. You will not realize that the accident had happened on the altered timeline because it did not. This results in the disappearance of the insatiable desire to change the undesirable results, which in turn, allows the original timeline to re-manifest in the next iteration, which has the fatal version of the accident, and so on…

The original timeline is set and will always reassert itself whenever possible. The end result is that you are accident-free every other iteration… A bit confusing, I know, but this is how it works.

Universal Consciousness

Let's look at why Universal consciousness is different from any other kind of consciousness and summarize its distinguishing features.

There are two major components to Universal consciousness, namely:

• Creative principle (Christ consciousness).

• Cosmic principle (Cosmic consciousness).

In turn, the Creative principle is divided into the following two components.

• Krishnic principle (Krishna consciousness).

• Buddhic principle (Buddha consciousness).

In Universal consciousness, we see the interplay of all these principles as being inseparable. This interplay and fusion of consciousness, as a single entity that gestalts far beyond its individual components is the most distinguishing feature of Universal consciousness.

If there is a deity, Universal consciousness could certainly be thought of as its mind...Consider for a moment that if you are created in the image of God, then it is not a great stretch of the imagination to understand that you are entitled to evolve into that image…

Definition

Universal consciousness can be defined as consciousness having the universal qualities of:

OMNISCIENCE - Defined as: having total knowledge. All-knowing.

OMNIPRESENCE - Defined as: Present everywhere simultaneously.

OMNIPOTENCE - Defined as: Having unlimited or universal power, authority, or force; all-powerful.

There is a caveat for each of the above. You can only be in, let's say, omniscience if you are all-knowing. As soon as you focus on a specific piece of information, you are no longer in that consciousness...however, there is a trick to this, which I will now cover.

The simple trick is to remain in, say, omniscience while answering questions. This will allow you to function as an oracle of sorts. Never knowing the question or answer beforehand, *often learning right along with the questioner...*

(The steps for reaching Universal consciousness are covered in the second part of this book).

Omniscience

My personal experience with Universal consciousness is the balancing act of simultaneously maintaining all three states, i.e., Omniscience, Omnipotence, and Omnipresence. I can sustain omniscience, for example, by *responding* to questions while maintaining a state of omniscience. As soon as I focus on any individual piece of information other than what was asked, I am no longer in Omniscience. In other words, I exist in a state of knowing nothing. I simply let answers flow through me, elicited by the questions, many times learning as they, the questioners, do.

Responding to a question elicits an automatic response from the reservoir of infinite knowledge.

OMNIPOTENCE

My experience with Omnipotence, is by existing in a state of powerlessness, where power is an integral given, imbuing me with the action of simple intention and visualization, manifests as Universal power, where a spoken word manifests as a creation. As soon as I try to direct my individual power, for physical reasons, I am no longer in a state of Universal power.

For example, let's say that I am concerned about the international state of nuclear saber-rattling. Issuing intentions from an Omnipotence state, affecting emotional statis, I can decrease world tension. However, let's say that I intend the self-destruction of a particularly bothersome nuclear arsenal, whether successful or not, would drop me out of Omnipotence.

Omnipresence

By consciously existing nowhere, I exist everywhere, in the state of Omnipresence... As soon as I consciously exist in any particular place, I am no longer in a state of Omnipresence, and as a result, I drop out of Universal Consciousness.

You, at the core of your being, spend a lot of time and energy pinpointing exactly where you are at any given moment. If you forget where you live, for example, you might wind up in a hospital or home.

However, while practicing Omnipresence, you are always safe because as soon as you feel fear, you are instantly returned to your everyday life...

A WAY OUTSIDE THE BOX

As we approach a state of Omnipresence, it is good to remember that many before you have attained this state in complete safety, and so will you...

Steps taken:

First, concentrate on exactly where you are located at this time.

Next, envision in your imagination that you are letting go of the idea that you exist at any particular place and that you are everywhere in the universe. In order to do this step properly, it is necessary to let go of your idea of where you are physically located. This step is mainly one of practice. It is best to practice at least once a day. I found the best time for me was just as I was going to sleep. It seemed easier to separate myself from my daily consciousness and move into a state of Omnipresence.

You will know, without a doubt, that you have attained Omnipresence once you have...

Manifesting all three states of Universal Consciousness equally, one finds oneself in a balanced state of Universal Consciousness... or God Consciousness... balanced like a three-legged stool… If you are having trouble understanding the above, that is OK. I would be amazed if you didn't! We will go over it in more detail as we progress.

This information is for humanity perhaps a thousand years in the future…It is being released now so it may percolate over time and will seem natural to the people in the future...

So, if it all seems a bit daunting, this is more than understandable. Just absorb what you can and know you are being guided by your higher power…As I mentioned before, treat this book more as a reference than as something one reads for entertainment…

Universal Consciousness perfectly combines all consciousnesses. This is because it manifested first as a unity (a universal concept that incorporates all consciousness), and then naturally subdivided into its constituent parts or sub-components.

For Universal Consciousness to function in the three-dimensional planes of duality (where you live), it had to be divided into two major principles, namely, Cosmic and Christ.

The Cosmic principle is the external universe, while the Christ principle represents the internal. These principles are equal and opposite. In this book, I will share some methods to help you reconstruct these two divergent principles back into Universal Consciousness in Part Two.

Why Is Universal Consciousness Important?

As one master the art of existing in a state of Universal, or God consciousness, there is an open-ended expansion of awareness, consisting of continuous epiphanies, that naturally expand exponentially. This is the result of a single point of consciousness expanding out into infinite potential, as compared to the static state of an infinite self, focusing down upon a single recipient consciousness.

Within mastery comes the naturally increasing ability to automatically manifest both methods simultaneously. That of a singularity to a multiplicity, combined with a multiplicity to a singularity…This is an example of a Master, student relationship, where the Master enlightens the student through a sharing of knowledge. This is imbued with the further expansion of awareness within the Master through the act of teaching, which can then be transmitted back to the student in a potentially never-ending aggregate of enlightenment…

This is better understood when viewed from the understanding that there is only one consciousness, existing within a self-perpetuating state, of ever-expanding self, into cosmic awareness…

As the whole expands in awareness, so do the dependent parts, which, in turn, further expands the whole…we could call this a perpetual universal gestalt...

Putting It All Together

I gathered all of the information contained in this book for you to understand and use now... Most of humanity will not understand it for, perhaps, a thousand years in the future…This highwire act is a lot easier than it sounds! As you float above omniscience, for example, visualize a questioner asking you a question. This questioner is a manifestation of an alternate you). You simply allow the answer to flow through you that is your omniscient self, without violating any of the rules, enabling you to ask and understand any question…If this is too hard to understand, then put it away for later study...

The current level of awareness for humanity is severely restricted.

(Understandable since we have only been at it for six thousand years out of our 25,000-year cycle. The earlier inhabitants, the Reptilians, shape-shifters, who had finished their 25,000-year cycle, were supposed to hand it off to us but in Trumpian fashion, were unwilling to let go. This is still a problem for us today).

(There are a group of powerful, advanced souls who are addicted to sex, power, and war, like players on a board game. (Ever played "Risk"?) The rest of us are simply window-dressing. They reincarnate as quickly as possible, usually in about a year, to grow up and continue the game. They are easy to spot. Just look at the world's dictators. These unfortunates have been referred to as "Fallen Angels." However, even they serve a purpose in the bigger picture).

Most people might not notice this restriction of awareness unless they compare it with others who are less restricted. Even then, the nature of these restrictions might prevent comparisons. Universal consciousness frees us from restrictions. Our hive-mindedness is structured to allow those who develop beyond the 'consumer state' the ability to rocket into the superhuman kingdom. Eventually, everyone will achieve this goal. And in one sense, already have… (The kingdoms are, as you know, Mineral, Plant, Insect, Animal, Human, and now, Superhuman...

Vibration

If you have ever watched water being subjected to vibration, you may have noticed a pattern that formed peaks and valleys. In this example, the valleys represent positive voids or a lack of water, and the peaks represent a negative abundance of water.

(The positive and negative model used here is in keeping with a battery where the positive pole represents fewer electrons, and the negative pole represents a plethora of electrons. The positive pole is hungry for electrons, while the negative pole is glad to give up its abundance, seeking balance).

Hydrogen Atom

Surrounding the nucleus and forming the outer portion of the ball is the densest part of the structure. (Counter-intuitive, I know). This is the rudimentary formation of a hydrogen atom. (And curiously, the exact shape of your universe). The inner core is the Proton, and the next layer is the encircling void, the second dimension, and the encircling dense energy is the first dimension. The result is a unipolar formation with the north pole trapped in its center and the dense outer shell existing as the south pole, which creates and forces into being the nucleus. This forcing together is the signature attribute of creation.

(See diagram below)

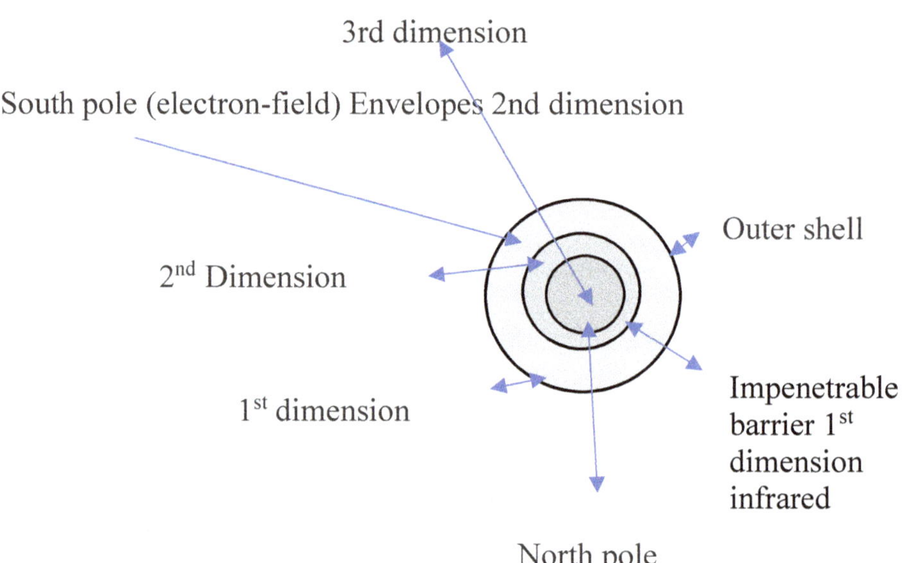

The manifestation of hydrogen and helium is universal in that there is nowhere within the closed sphere that composes our universe that is unaffected. With hydrogen and helium, there is an accompanying universal rise in temperature because of increasing vibration via heat generated by protons and the subsequent occurring motion and rudimentary time.

The Big Bang?

(Below are some of my thoughts about what kind of universe we live in. Admittedly vastly different from 'modern theory,' however, it is some of what I have observed over many years of exploring the past. I wanted to share it with you to reframe and broaden your viewpoint if you wish..).

In this model of the universe, there is NO Big Bang. What we observe is a quiet, static universe that, although in motion, is not expanding and, in fact, cannot expand because it is contained inside an impenetrable sphere.

Redshift

(Below are my thoughts on why modern theory thinks what it does and why it may be mistaken).

There is something called the "Red Shift." What this means is when light is moving away from us, its frequency moves towards the lower end of vibration. Remember hearing a train blowing its horn? As it approaches, the sound of the horn is higher than after it passes, when it sounds noticeably lower.

The same is true for light. Light approaching us shifts toward the higher end of the spectrum, known as the blue shift).

(The reverse is also true. When light is moving away from us, its frequency is 'red shifted' toward the lower end of the visible spectrum.

In my estimation, modern theory is mistaken. The mistake began with observations of red-shifted stars and galaxies appearing as though everything was moving away from us as though we were lepers. The farther away, the more red-shifted it is and, therefore, the faster it moves, or so the theory goes.

A Different Theory

(DISCLAIMER. DO NOT TRY THE EXPERIMENT BELOW…SERIOUS DAMAGE MAY OCCUR TO YOUR EYES!)

In the 1970s, I noticed that when observing a reflection of the sun for a fraction of a second, it left an image on my retina after I closed my eyes. First was a bright white ball that devolved into successively lower frequency colors: violet, purple, indigo, blue, green, orange, finally reaching red. It occurred to me that this might be what was happening to light as it traveled immense distances to reach our telescopes. Over time, light loses its higher frequency content, dropping into the lower, longer wavelength frequencies, replicating a 'redshift.' The farther away the object, the more red-shifted it would appear.

Excited, wanting to confirm my theory, I went to a nearby university, where I asked a physics professor if my theory could be possible. He was quick to step on my idea, claiming that light would degenerate in amplitude but certainly not in content.

I was not discouraged, figuring the guy probably never had an original thought. I put my theory on the back burner for a later date, which turned out to be decades later.

Summary

Current theory has light shifting toward the red end of the spectrum, denoting stars moving away from us. The farther away they are, the faster they recede. They concluded that this must mean that the universe is expanding, and out of this was born the Big Bang.

I believe that contrary to current theory, white light degenerated over time, giving the false impression that it was 'red-shifted.' *I read that another brave soul recently published the same theory. His idea was mockingly called "Tired Light."* (The theory was conceived of by Fritz Zwicky in 1929 as an alternative to the expanding universe theory).

It is tough to be on the front line of academia...I am so glad I am not on it! Author

Interestingly, the redshift could determine how distant a galaxy might be. The more red-shifted, the farther away, allowing us to accurately measure the distance to each galaxy...

"Are there 'blue-shifted' galaxies observed?" Yes, about one hundred, *all being <u>close</u> to our galaxy.*

Speed Of Light

In our continuing observation of the universe and to round out your viewpoint, it is prudent to discuss the speed of light.

From all that I have observed, it is evident to me that light propagates through the invisible energy that pervades our universe. The speed of light tells a lot about this energy.

Light excites the invisible medium, causing a ball of disturbance to move out into the universe at the speed of light. The ball expands until it reaches us and beyond. In fact, it bounces off the boundaries of our enclosed universe, causing all sorts of future optical problems for astronomers.

To travel faster than the speed of light, the vehicle cannot be dependent upon the same medium that light uses.

Refesher

THE TWELVE FACES OF GOD

Physical Bodies

The chart below is composed of information very carefully gathered. It is not simply a repeat of the same old system left over from many centuries ago. As such, be aware that it is an entirely different system based upon entirely different criteria. I mention this to prepare you for the possible confusion that this information might bring, not corresponding to what you have previously learned and, perhaps, even teach. If you recall, Jesus had trouble teaching the New Message for the "New Age," just two thousand years ago. And although I, as a modern metaphysical teacher, am not physically crucified, there is a ubiquitous tendency to ignore me, which, sadly, turns a challenging task into an improbable one.

New Metaphysics

The old "Seven Chakra System," while still valid, was released to the general population expressly for the 2000-year period that just finished. For the same reason, now, the "Twelve Chakra System" is being released into the general population, expressly for the next 2000-year period, known as the "Orange Age."

Each Age brings with it new and appropriate information and people to disseminate it. It is more than incumbent upon the metaphysical leaders and teachers to be the first to learn the "New Metaphysics," so that, obviously, they may integrate it with their knowledge of the "Old Metaphysics."

In addition to helping you come into a measure of Cosmic Consciousness, a thorough study of the individual component bodies that make up the composite human being will increase and promote understanding of how the human complex works, and thus bring the healing arts one step closer to replacing the pharmaceutical gridlock in which medical practice now exists. It is to this end that I share the following observations: At a certain level of Cosmic Consciousness, the human body is "seen,," as consisting of twelve separate bodies, divided by rates of vibration. These bodies are divided into three groups of four. The densest group of the four is the Physical group.

Visualize a ball of energy. The outermost ball vibrates at infrared (Aries). Moving inward, the next ball is a brownish red (Taurus). The next ball is burgundy (Virgo)., and finally, an orange ball (Capricorn).

See the diagram below.

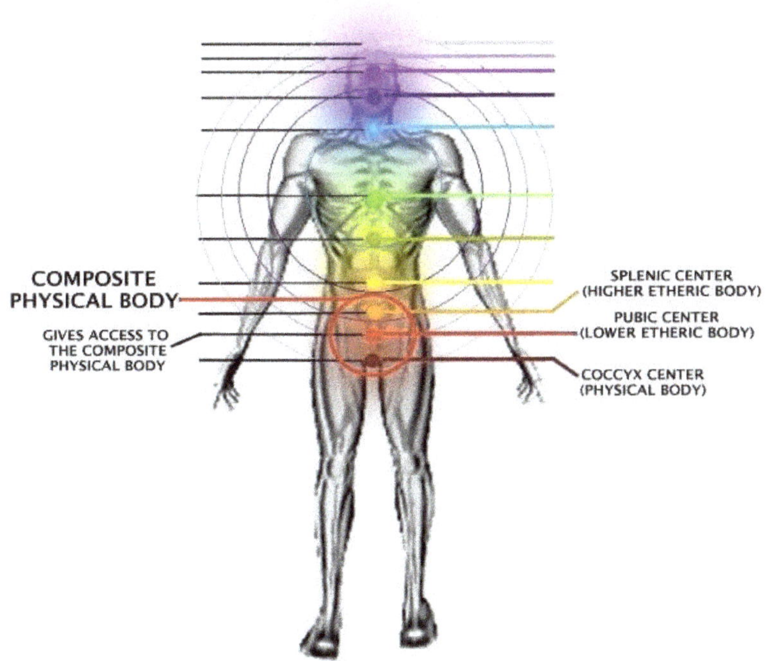

The physical body is composed of four separate bodies, each superimposed and existing within the same relative space, separated only by degrees of vibration. There is, of course, the outer physical shell or "Meat" body, with which you are most familiar. This is your densest body. This "vehicle" interfaces with three-dimensional space and allows us to experience the outer world. It is a hard shell that protects us from the outside, and has a relationship to your Soul, the way your car has a relationship with you.

In the diagram above, we see the various Chakras, or energy centers, that interface with each corresponding body.

Starting with the physical body (Taurus), like Russian nesting dolls, each higher vibratory body exists inside of the previous body.

Although called the 12-chakra system, we only count eleven chakras in either a man or a woman. (We will examine the illusive Aries, infrared, in a later section).

The Physical body, by itself, has no personality or motivation other than to eat and sleep. If you have ever visited a "rest home," you may have seen cases of extremely elderly people who fit this description. These are cases of the astral bodies dying before the physical body.

The Lower Etheric Body

Existing inside of your densest "Physical Body," there are two more physical bodies. They walk around with you when you walk around. You may think you do not know about them, but you do.

The next densest body to your "Physical Body," is your "Sexual" Body. In Germany, it is called the "Doppelganger" or Double. Here, it is called the "Etheric Double" or the "Lower Etheric Body." It is the vibratory center of the "Physical Body," and it contains your personality and is primarily concerned with procreation. In sexually active people, this center has a great deal to do with their activities. Singles Bars or singles chat rooms on the Internet attract this body. It is usually extremely interested in the physical attributes of the opposite sex. Hollywood has capitalized on the sexual charisma of great personalities.

This, the "Lower Etheric Body," charges up at night when you are asleep by rising about six inches above your physical body. If you have ever gotten overly tired and started to doze off, you might have experienced the unpleasant sensation of suddenly jumping awake, as though there was a loud noise or explosion? This was your Etheric Body prematurely exiting (to replenish the life force) before you were completely asleep. This startles your physical body (that would normally be asleep), which, in turn, causes your Etheric Body to "crash" back into you, jarring you awake. You may have also experienced a state of paralysis, where no matter how hard you tried, you could not move or speak. This also might have been accompanied by the sound of rushing wind. (Or, in the most severe cases, a series of explosions that might resemble a seizure). This is the beginning of what is called Etheric Projection. The next time this happens, you could calm yourself and let the experience happen...

It is a valuable experience to have, in that it very quickly turns skeptics into believers. (If you have never had these experiences, it does not matter, for although interesting, it is not necessary for your present progress and, in fact, can become an addictive distraction).

If a Soul is un-evolved or unusually interested in the sexual activities of others, then its interest through the lower Etheric body can become a problem for it. In this time period, this was quite common. It is the combination of the Lower and Higher Etheric bodies that produce what we call Ghosts. (This combination of Etheric bodies can last for many years, even though they have long been discarded by the Soul).

As we mature, we become more in tune with our higher vibratory bodies. The hormone levels that control our sexual activity lessen and allow us to discover the more discreet portions of our minds and spirits. People who feel they have died sexually have developed a form of apathy in this body. Also, people who have a flat and uninteresting personality may suffer from an underdeveloped or damaged sexual body.

As a point of interest, it is the lower etheric plane where extra-terrestrials seem to thrive, accounting for many, if not all, close encounters...

The Higher Etheric Body

Next is the last of the three, the "Higher Etheric Body." It is the color of an orange blossom. It processes the life force that enables you to be healthy and alive...

Health Issues

The health of the Higher Etheric body is extremely important to the general health and vitality of your entire being. It was mistakenly thought to be the sexual body, in women, by eastern mystics, because when it shut down, it also shut down the sex drive, and when a healer activated it, it occasionally resulted in spontaneous orgasm. It is located between the navel and the sexual center and is associated with the spleen. For this reason, it is sometimes called the "Splenic Center."

Unfortunately, most women who work in the business place with men, shut this center down. This forms a sort of psychic chastity belt, and can cause premature sexual shutdown, (by promoting less hormonal activity), and general health problems.

A Review Of The More Important Points:

The "Physical Body" is made up of four separate bodies.

Each body occupies the same physical space, but each vibrates at a different rate of vibration.

Although the three bodies work in tandem to function as the "Physical Body," they can be separated, and can operate independently. (Upon the death of the outer physical shell, which usually, dies first, it is the combination of the Lower and Higher Etheric bodies that make ghosts).

Below is a quick review of the physical bodies.

1. The densest body forms the outer "meat" shell. It is your work horse. It interfaces with the external three-dimensional universe.
2. The next less dense body is the "Sexual," (or "Lower Etheric body") that contains a portion of the indwelling Self, in the form of the Personality. Its color is burgundy.
3. The last of the three physical bodies is the least dense, and the highest in vibration. It is the "Higher Etheric body," also referred to as the "Astral Body." It is this body that is responsible for processing the life force (orange energy) that animates the "Physical Body."

The Twelve Faces Of God
Physical Bodies - Cont.

All the Physical Bodies we have looked at, (as well as the Mental and Emotional bodies we will study in subsequent lessons), are related to a specific part of the spectrum as a color, and are also related to either the Sun, or a Planet within our Solar System, and a particular Sign of the Zodiac. This knowledge was perfectly understood by the Ancients and represents the parent system for all subsequent astrological systems but has been very watered down and refined over the Ages into the form you see today, losing most of its original importance as relates to a method for unlocking the secrets to our true nature. I believe the work done by these ancient metaphysical giants to be extremely valuable, and it is with this in mind that I have revived the original knowledge and share it with you, as it was originally meant to be understood.

Before you became involved in "time" and the physical universe, you shared your Soul with your other half. Upon entering the plane of duality, the two of you were separated. There is an intense desire in both of you to reunite. Although you and your mate, as male and female, have the same number of centers (chakras) within your physical bodies, the emphasis, due to polarities, are different. In this lesson you will look at some of these differences.

The diagram (See below), is not meant to be an exact representation of the human aura. It is, instead, meant to emphasize the basic differences, in the purest sense, between a man and a woman. Notice that the man has only three dominate centers, consisting of the three Fire Signs: Aries-infrared, Leo-yellow, and Sagittarius-indigo, while a woman has eleven...

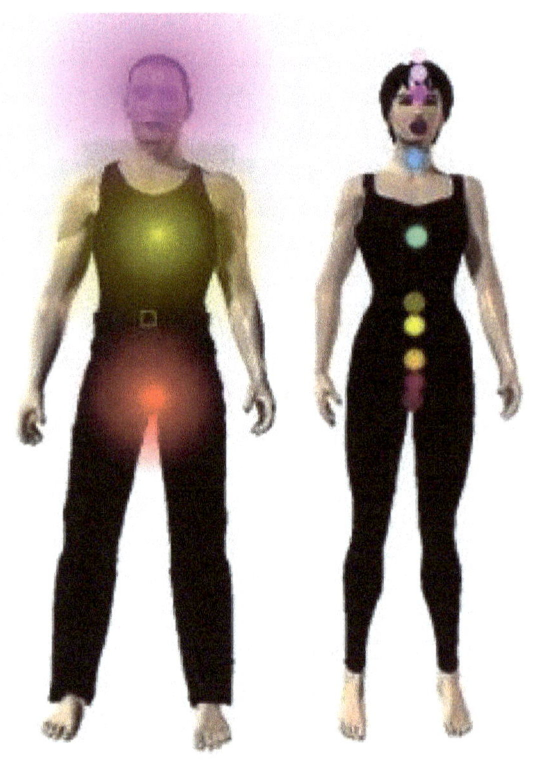

MAN AND WOMAN

You can see at once the profound differences in the fundamental predominant access to chakras. The female is infinitely more sensitive, whereas the man is almost a blunt instrument.

In this book, I will show you how to access all of the centers. And how to transcend them to access Cosmic Consciousness, on your way to Universal Consciousness. (That is if you are not too afraid to venture so far from your comfort zone…Smiling). Anyway, just read through the material. The information that is pertinent to you will stand out and help you to move to the next step in your evolution…

In the chart below, you can see how the differences between a man and a woman originates. The white globe at the top represents pure potential in the primordial second-dimension, (Christ principle), before its decent into the planes of duality. Notice that it sub-divides into a trinity consisting of red, yellow, and indigo globes. This combination represents the male principle. Below this are further sub-divisions representing the female principle. In our current discussion we are focusing on the physical portion of the male trinity (the red globe, Aries), and its component sub-divisions, (brown, burgundy and orange globes as Taurus, Virgo and Capricorn, respectively).

In the diagram below, we start with a white globe on top. It represents several things: It is white light, the fifth dimension and the Christ. It represents everything in creation, including you and me. White light is comprised of three components: Infrared, Yellow, and Indigo. (This is different than your television, which is red, green, and blue).

Each of these are Fire signs. They are subdivided into three subdivisions each. Notice the numbering system.

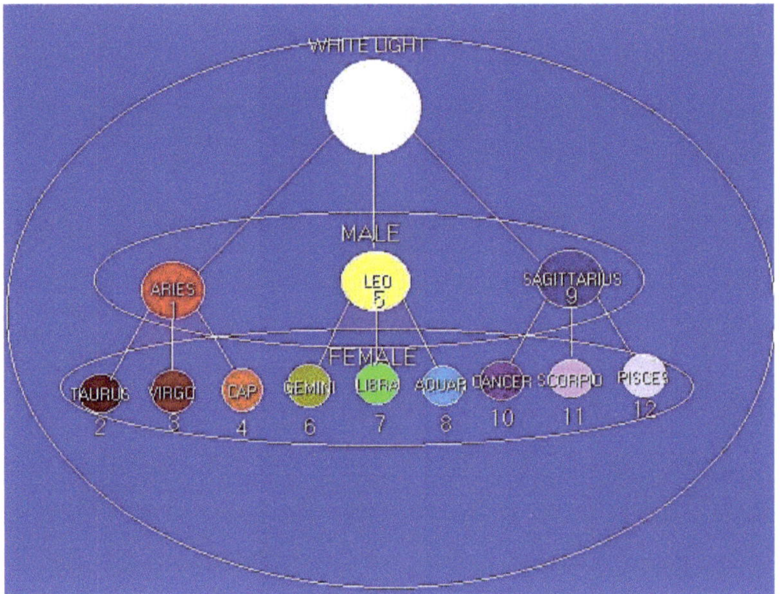

CHART OF SIGNS

Another way to look at the chart above is to consider the "white globe" as our Sun. The trinity, consisting of the three "Fire Signs," represents the three component principles of the Sun: namely, "outward expansion," represented by "Aries" (3D); "inward collapsation," represented by "Sagittarius" (4D); and lastly, the "static state," represented by "Leo" (5D). This leaves the nine remaining "Signs," which represent the nine planets, starting with "Taurus," whose planet is "Mercury," and ending with "Pisces," whose planet was "Pluto."

I realize that this is different from what is currently thought, but please understand that these designations only serve to place each of these "Signs," as vibratory principles, into their proper positions in relation to the Sun and are not dependent upon there being any planets at all. The astrological systems currently in vogue are based upon the "magnetic" positions and influences of heavenly bodies upon the Earth, and subsequently upon you. The system you are studying now is based upon the "vibrational" sub-structure of the Solar System.

This system manifests as a macrocosmic pattern, which is also found in human beings as a microcosmic sub-structure, and has nothing to do with magnetic influence or the positions of the planets.

You learned in the last excerpt that the physical body can be separated into three components. This can be thought of as four separate bodies: the three separate component bodies and the fourth, which is the non-separated, composite body that functions as a totality. It is this composite body functioning as a totality that we will look at first.

The composite physical body, as with all the bodies we will study, can be identified with a color in the spectrum. The color for the composite physical body is usually thought of as bright red, although it extends from infrared up through the visible range of red.

The Sign of the zodiac with which the composite physical body is identified is the Sign of "Aries," the Ram. Aries, a "Fire Sign," represents the outward expansion of energy from the Sun and is the abstract representation of the lower vibratory range of physical form. It also manifests as male sexual energy, known as Kundalini (this is different from current theory, which identifies it as female energy).

In line with my theories, Aries, as a Fire Sign, is associated with the Sun, and not Planet Mars, as is held in modern Astrology. Aries is also associated with the shell of infrared energy that extends out from the Sun, and encompasses the three inner planets, Mercury, Venus, and Earth. As was mentioned before, the system you are presently learning has nothing to do with Astrology, or Astrological influences, so please do not let the differences confuse you. They are two completely different systems, founded upon an entirely different basis. Only the names of the "Signs," and their general characteristics are the same.

I have included the astrological signs for those of you who are familiar with them, in the hopes that it might provide more clarity...

Although both males and females have a "composite physical body," there are some differences. The "composite" physical body is considered more as the "male" polarization, in relation to the three "component" bodies, which are considered as the "female" polarization. "Aries" as a center (chakra) is the "Male Sexual Center."

Emotionally "red" is identified with rage, on one end of the red spectrum, and courage on the other, and is responsible for the saying "seeing red." Red is also the color seen in the aura near the area of an injury. In the art of energy manipulation, red is a principle healing color. Several vibratory states of red indicate sexual interest or arousal...

(Most domestic animals I have looked at appear to have a permanent red aura).

It is important to note that the component body, known as the Sexual Body, (although both males and females have one), is known as the Female Sexual Center, (burgundy). This is because the male sexual center resides in the composite body, (red), rather than in the principal component body where the female sexual center resides.

The first of the three component bodies comprising the composite physical body is the Physical "Meat" Body. Here, you can see the physical differences in polarization between male and female. This body, whether it is male or female, is identified with the Earth Sign "Taurus *the Bull*" and is related to the "Coccyx Center" at the base of the spine. Its color is associated with the vibratory part of the visible spectrum that is dark red or brown.

Taurus represents the first kingdom, the "Mineral Kingdom," and is related to the vibrating shell of energy encircling the Sun, which extends out to just beyond the vicinity of the planet Mercury, the planet with which it is associated.

The next body you will learn about is the Sexual Body (or your Etheric Body). Although both males and females have one, it is considered the Female Sexual Center. It is identified by a spectral color that is burgundy. This color in the human aura indicates feelings of lasciviousness. The diagram below is a representation of the assorted colors associated with the human aura. The major difference between a man and a woman is that the "Sexual Center" is "red" in the man and "burgundy" in the woman.

The Sign of the zodiac associated with this center is the Earth Sign "Virgo." It is vibrationally connected with the shell of energy encircling the Sun, which extends out to just beyond the vicinity of the planet Venus, the planet with which this body is aptly associated, and represents the second kingdom, the "Plant Kingdom."

This body is used in what is called bilocation—the ability to be in two places at the same time. The practitioner can instantaneously transport their sexual body to any distance. Once there, they can, by an effort of will, lower the vibrations of this body so that it may be seen and even interacted with. This was brought to an art by a few Yogi Adepts from the Far East.

Empathic ability relies upon being able to detach this body and overlay or merge it with another person's physical body (while the practitioner remains awake) for the purpose of healing. This ability can be learned and is indispensable for those of us who are involved in the Healing Arts. You can tell if you are empathetically inclined by whether you can feel another's illness. *Distance seems not to matter. I have interacted with students in other countries instantaneously.*

(For example, if you are around someone who has trouble breathing, do you suddenly feel as though you are having trouble breathing? You may have been told that you have a big imagination or that you are a hypochondriac. *The truth is that you are a budding empath.*)

The last physical body you will look at is the "Higher Etheric." This, too, is considered a female polarity and is associated with the Earth Sign "Capricorn the *Goat.*" Its spectral color is orange. An orange color, when observed in the human aura, denotes distinct kinds of pride, depending upon the shade. Darker shades indicate hurt pride, while lighter shades indicate pride of ownership or accomplishment. A proud father will exhibit a very bright orange.

This is the color of the life force, or vital energy, and, because it is connected to the "Insect Kingdom," it has a great deal to do with the nature to organize and socialize. *The* Higher Etheric *is associated with the vibrating shell of energy encircling the Sun,* which *extends out to just beyond the vicinity of the planet Earth, the planet with which this body is associated, and represents the third kingdom, the "Insect Kingdom."*

(As a note of interest, because of orange energy and its role as the life force necessary to produce sentience, this would indicate the presence of physical life-forms exclusively on the third planet from the Sun. This could very well be a part of our Sun's "signature" that it sends out to other Solar Systems, encoded in its radiant energy we call light.)

THE TWELVE FACES OF GOD

Mental Bodies

Residing within and above the physical, (in terms of vibration) is the "Mental Body," which deals with planning and abstract thinking. The color for the composite mental body is bright yellow. Like the Physical Body, it is also made up of three separate bodies, the first of which is the "Lower Mental Body" or "lower mind." This is the beginning of what is called the "Mental Plane." Here we are concerned with the facts of the world. It is a lightning-fast computer. Although this body is associated with the Animal-kingdom, it has highly evolved in Man.

Idiot Savants and child geniuses exhibit some of the amazing abilities available in a sufficiently developed Lower Mental Body. Its color is golden yellow.

Note, it is amazing to me that we are taught starting as children, and continuing through higher education, how not to use our brain...

The next higher body in vibration, is the "Higher Mental Body." This is the mental body that most of Mankind is striving to master. Here we are learning how to apply judgment and powers of discrimination. The better Generals throughout world history had a highly developed Higher Mental Body. This faculty will be exceptionally developed in the

Superhuman Kingdom, which will give us the ability to understand the many subterfuges so prevalent in politics and business of the time.

This was an Age when the Masters of deceit flourished, and the ability to lie and deceive was rewarded with power and wealth! The general population was not able to discriminate, and therefore were fair game to the craftier predators among them. Unfortunately, some of the more advance among us, because of their advanced powers of discrimination, became caught up in this process as predators, which produced internal conflict within their highly developed spiritual and moral bodies.

The highest vibrational Mental Body is the "Intuitive Body." This faculty gives the user the ability to "know" without knowing. In the present time, advanced Man was beginning to learn to use this body.

A Review Of The More Important Points

The Mental Body resides upon the various Mental planes of existence and is concerned with the mental abilities and qualities of the mind.

It is composed of three separate bodies.

Each body occupies the same physical space, but each vibrates at a different rate of vibration.

Although the three bodies work in tandem to function, they remain separated by vibration.

The lowest, in vibration, is the Lower Mental Body. It is like a calculator. It resides on the lowest mental plane. (The Mental Plane represents divisions and subdivisions of the Mental Body).

The second part of the Mental Body is the Higher Mental Body. It is the central part that contains a portion of the indwelling "Self," in the form of the Ego.

The last mental body is the Intuitive Body. It has the highest vibration. It bestows the faculty of intuition (or knowing without knowing). Very few people of today have developed this faculty to any degree. Numbering among those who have, are many Psychics, Mystics and, of course, Aquarians.

Each of the mental bodies you have just learned about is related harmonically to a specific part of the spectrum as a color, and is also related to either the Sun, or a Planet within our Solar system, and a sign of the Zodiac. Although, on the inner planes, the Mental Body appears to reside in simply a higher vibratory level from the physical, it has a multidimensional placement that is in the center of your being. As was stated earlier, the mental body is a composite of three mental bodies. It is associated with the Fire Sign "Leo the Lion." Its polarization is male and represents the "Male Heart Center." Although it extends, in the human body, from above the throat to below the solar plexus, it is accessed through the lower portion of the solar plexus. It is here we find a kind of animal courage or aggression.

The Composite Mental Body

The Composite Mental Body is yellow, (bright yellow) and in the context of mentality, is associated with pure intellect. It represents the abstract mind. Leo is also associated, as the central vibratory reflection of the Sun, with the shell of vibrating energy that encompasses the three central planets, Mars, Jupiter, and Saturn. Leo, a Fire sign, represents the central consciousness of the Sun.

The Lower Mental Body

The Mental Body is made up of three component bodies, the first of which is the "Lower Mental Body." This body is the color of dark yellow (male, mental) or pink (female, emotion). It is this pink color that is responsible for the saying "sees through rose-colored glasses." This pink vibration causes its practitioner to live in a fairy land of wonderfulness, a hard reality to maintain in today's world. Marilyn Monroe is an example of a pink Gemini. A certain shade of pink is associated with the feelings of puppy dog love.

The Lower Mental Body is associated with the Air Sign, "Gemini the twins." In terms of birds, this air sign is most akin to the hawk. (Some Geminis look like birds of prey, with pronounced hawk-like features).

The vibratory shell, for the Lower mental Body, extends out from the Sun to the vicinity of the planet Mars. Physically, it is accessed through the upper half of the Solar Plexus, and represents the upper echelon of the fourth kingdom, the "Animal kingdom." Domestic animals usually have this center well developed. It is here we get feelings of right and wrong. It is also where we get a "gut" feeling about things. It is in this area of the Solar Plexus that we feel the numbing fear that is the opposite of courageousness, and this is the reason the term "yellow" (dark yellow) is associated with cowardliness.

Because of widespread abuse and killing of animals, all over the world, we are affected through sympathetic vibrations in this body, causing us to have unwarranted feelings of fear in some of the more sensitive of us. This is also the body where the feelings of shame are experienced.

The Higher Mental Body

Next is the "Higher Mental Body." This body is composed of all shades of green, the midway point of all the colors. This is the "Female Heart Center," and is associated with the Air Sign, "Libra the Scales."

Libra as an air sign is akin to an owl. Many Male Librans of this type will look a bit like an owl.

Libra represents the center or balance point of the spectrum. Its planetary connection is the vibrating shell of energy that extends out from the Sun to the vicinity of the planet Jupiter, the fifth and most central planet out of the nine, and represents the fifth kingdom, the Human Kingdom. Libra houses the Ego and is rigidly centered in its green habitat. On the negative side is where all manner of selfishness originates. It is also responsible for the saying, "green with envy."

The darker the shade of green the more intensely selfish. As you move through the darker shades, you find such old favorites as greed and vanity, not to mention avarice. It is no accident that our paper money is green. The lighter the shade, the more philanthropic, and in the central shades you find tranquility. There is a certain emotional openness in the lighter shades of green, within the Female Heart Center, that prompts the saying "wears her heart on her sleeve." (In the extremely light shades we find superficiality and frivolousness) Since Libra is the balance point, it gives the Human Being an <u>extra viewpoint</u> over the animal kingdom.

The animal has only four viewpoints, which results in emotionally based decisions. "This or that," "black or white." The Human Kingdom has five viewpoints. It is this extra viewpoint that allows a detached reference point that gives the ability to discriminate or discern. This results in intellectually based decisions and is one of the primary differences between animal and human behavior.

One of the problems with this body, for the inept, is the inability to decide. Because of the capability of seeing all sides of a decision as being equal, it becomes difficult to make any decisions at all. This type of person does not like to argue because they can understand and sympathize with both sides equally. Certain types of mental illness derive from the negative aspects of this body, in the form of procrastination, in combination with fear found in the upper solar plexus, usually experienced as a gone feeling. Agoraphobia (fear of open spaces) and other kinds of phobias in this category can produce a paralysis of fear.

Color therapy can diminish, if not completely cure, most of these types of debilitating phobias. (Infrared is greens complementary color).

In men, the sign of Libra makes for excellent Generals, as an example, General Eisenhower.

The Intuitional Body

The last Mental Body is the Intuitional Body. This body has, as its vibrational color base, all shades of blue and is accessed through the throat center. It is associated with the Air Sign "Aquarius, the Water Bearer." Many people think it is a water sign because of this, but it is the highest vibrational Air Sign. It is here the saying "feeling blue" comes from. The darker the shades of blue, the more serious the mood, which can produce feelings of melancholia. The lighter the shades of blue can evoke feelings of spiritual devotion. The highest shades of blue denote the highest feelings of altruism, inspiration, and selflessness. However, this can be a problem for the practitioner, as they can easily be victimized or taken advantage of.

The planetary connection for the Intuitional Body is the vibrating shell of energy that extends out from the Sun to the vicinity of the planet Saturn and represents the sixth kingdom, the "Superhuman Kingdom." The Intuitional Body, an Air Sign, is most like the eagle.

Aloofness or cold loftiness can be a problem for this body. Feelings of sympathy emanating from the Intuitional Body at the throat center are responsible for the saying that one is "choked up." Additionally, fear emanating from the upper solar plexus can sometimes cause this center to shut down, which is why you might have difficulty speaking when you are scared.

Although intuition is this body's strong point, it can be dangerous by itself. This is the origin of the saying, "fools rush in where angels fear to tread." The lightest blue type of Aquarian can also vie with the pink Gemini for the title of "airhead." The lighter shades of blue produce a feeling, in those around them, of trustworthiness and good-naturedness.

The addition of intuition to the Human Being gives him six separate viewpoints. This distinction is the difference between the Human Being, and the "Superhuman Being," that is coming into being over the next several million years. A difference as great as that between the human

and the domesticated animal...

THE TWELVE FACES OF GOD
Emotional/Spiritual Bodies

The Spiritual Body, represented by Sagittarius, resides within the same space as the Mental Plane but above it in terms of vibration. It is also a composite body, made up of three separate bodies. This body represents male emotions and female spirituality, which is extremely interesting because it vibrates in resonance with the color indigo. Indigo, when viewed clairvoyantly, appears almost black and is a virtual void. This means that, fundamentally, while experiencing the Spiritual Body, men exist in an emotional void, and women exist in a spiritual one.

Since the blackness of the void is much too severe for us as human beings to tolerate (at this time), indigo is nature's way of imitating the void without having to use it. The result for us is the same. It is necessary for us to experience nothingness to cause us to let go completely. This is a major and necessary developmental component at the highest level of human evolution.

The Spiritual Body is comprised of three component bodies, the first of which is the Volitional Body. This is the center of willpower and focus. Some of the greatest leaders throughout history have developed this faculty. In the male polarization, it is the "Eye of the Tiger" sought by combatants.

At certain levels of vibration, the Volitional Body (emotionally) can be a place of deep suicidal depression for the uninitiated. If you can see colors around people (auras), this depressed condition appears as a dark purple band around the eyes, giving the bizarre feeling that you are looking at a masked bandit or a raccoon. This condition can be quickly alleviated by color therapy, namely by concentrating on the color orange.

Here is something you can try if you feel depressed: meditate upon or gaze at a bright orange object or light (not too bright or for too long if it is a light source). This will lighten your aura and provide a measure of immediate relief.

Remember that men can be susceptible to the emotional effects of the Volitional Body, just as women can use it for focus and willpower to become top athletes. The Volitional Body is currently very underdeveloped in most of the world population.

The next highest vibrational vehicle is the Spiritual Cognitive Body. It is the place where spiritual knowledge is known. It conveys to the user great wisdom and clairvoyant powers. It is the central part, or heart, of the Spiritual Body and contains a portion of the indwelling "Self" in the form of the discrete Super Ego (an extension of the Soul). Our greatest spiritual teachers had access to this faculty. Emotionally, this body expresses spiritual power. Taken to extremes, it can produce megalomania, or what is known as a God complex.

The highest vibrational Spiritual Body, and the last in line, is the Guardian or Prudent Body. This body interfaces with the spiritual, or Fourth Dimensional "outside," just the way our physical outer shell interfaces with the Third Dimensional "outside." It filters out unnecessary or unwanted spiritual influences.

It is also a regulatory body, in that it moderates the amount of spiritual energy flowing into the lower vibrational vehicles, which regulates the amount of inspiration a person may have. If you are uninspired, this body may be asleep or has become damaged through psychic attack or drug abuse.

It can be awakened by direct energy manipulation at the most central spot on the top of the head. Sometimes this body, for some reason, (many times drug related) goes into overwhelm, and begins to produce an inordinate amount of fear. This, in turn, shuts down the spiritual flow through the system. In severe cases, this can result in a form of severe paranoia, agoraphobia, or even violent behavior. This is especially true for long-term cocaine, or heroin users, and short-term crystalline methamphetamine, (crystal meth), users. Sometimes, a single trip on lysergic acid will cause this body to go into permanent shutdown.

A Review Of The More Important Points-2

The "Spiritual Body" is made up of three separate bodies. Each body occupies the same physical space, but each vibrates at a distinctly different rate.Although the three bodies work in tandem to function as the "Spiritual Body," they can be separated and can operate independentlyThe first and lowest vibrational vehicle is the Volitional Body. It functions as a lens for focus and willpower but can have a negative emotional influence. The next, less dense body is the Spiritual Cognitive Body. It provides access to universal knowledge. The last of the three bodies is the least dense and the highest in vibration. It is the Prudent Body. It spiritually protects the lower bodies and controls the flow of spiritual energy.

Zodiacal Connections

Each of the spiritual bodies you have just learned about is related to a specific part of the spectrum as a color and is also related to either the Sun or a planet within our Solar System, as well as a sign of the Zodiac. As was stated earlier, the spiritual body is a composite of three spiritual bodies. It is associated with the Fire Sign Sagittarius, the Archer.

The Spiritual/Emotional Body is made up of three component bodies, the first of which is the Volitional Body, a center of creativity, will, and emotional power. It is located at the Between the Eyes Center, also referred to as the Third Eye. This center is associated with the pineal gland. The pineal gland is a small organ, about the size of a grain of rice, attached by a stalk to the posterior wall of the third ventricle of the brain. This is towards the back and above the cerebellum. It is called the pineal gland because it is shaped like a small pinecone.

The Volitional Body has the spectral vibration of purple. It is associated with the Water Sign Cancer, the Crab. Its planetary connection is the vibrating shell of energy in the vicinity of Uranus.

The next Spiritual Center is the Spiritual Cognitive Body. It is located at the Crown Center (or the Thousand-Petaled Lotus). It is associated with the Water Sign Scorpio. Its planetary connection is the vibrating shell of energy that extends out from the Sun to the vicinity of Neptune. Its color is violet. It is also associated with the billions of cells that comprise the physical brain, which, in this connection, is a facsimile of our Galaxy, the Milky Way, with its billions of stars. Scorpio is associated with the eyes. You may have heard the expression "Scorpio eyes." It is very distinctive, and once you have identified it, you will be able to spot them easily.

The Crown Center may seem like an unlikely place for Scorpio, which is usually associated with the sexual center. It is the only triple sign in the Zodiac, traditionally represented by the Eagle, the Snake, and the Scorpion. In the system you are learning about, Scorpio also has three centers. The first is its own center, the Crown Center, a wellspring of great emotional and spiritual power, which is the male spiritual center.

Next is the Female Heart Center, under Libra, a place of great intellectual capacity. Thirdly, there is the Female Sexual Center, under Virgo, sometimes called the "Little King" in men and sometimes connected with the "little professor" aspect of the personality. This is where you find the "know-it-all."

It becomes apparent that Scorpio is highly involved with Christ Consciousness, in that these centers represent three out of four of the manifestations of the Christ. Only Leo is missing. It is unfortunate that many Scorpios are fascinated with the least virtuous part of their nature.

The last center is the Prudent Body. It is associated with the Water Sign Pisces. Its color is ultraviolet or grey. Ultraviolet is the highest spiritual vibratory color within a human being. Grey is the spiritual color of fear. This aspect of fear is remarkably interesting in Pisces. This is not the usual animal fear you are most familiar with, that emerges from the solar plexus, it is, instead, the kind of fear called dread, or mortal fear, or experienced as the sometimes-paralyzing fear of the unknown. Fear is the regulatory device that the Prudent Body uses to control all the rest of the bodies. In this sense, the Prudent Body is a combination of all the rest of the bodies. However, this is a place from which great wisdom and diplomacy is born. It can be said that this body is the "Jack of all trades," but master of none.

The center for the Prudent Body is at the very top and center of the head and is called the Top of the Head Center. Its' planetary connection is the vibrating shell of energy in the vicinity of the planet Pluto. This center is usually associated with the pituitary gland.

Associations On The Head
Between Signs And Organs

HERE IS SOME INFORMATION THAT FEW, IF ANY, KNOW:

Pisces is associated with the ears and is dependent on hearing in order to learn. It must sound right. "Can't believe my ears." Even when Pisces is reading, for example, an internal voice will enunciate each word. From personal experience.

Scorpio, as most know, is associated with the eyes. And things must look right. "Something doesn't look right."

Cancer is associated with the nose. Things must smell right. "This whole thing stinks!" "something smells rotten in Denmark."

And Sagittarius. Is associated with the mouth. Things must taste, right. "Leaves a bad taste in my mouth.

PART THREE

Tying Up Loose Ends
beginning of the cycle

(I am glad to see that you are still with me...smiling)

In our continuing quest to understand the universe, the best place to start is the beginning of a cycle of creative manifestation. (The Universe seems to come and go at regular intervals).

At this point, we have the perfect set of circumstances to observe exactly how the universe comes into being. If you will permit me, I will bring you along with me as we observe.

• FIRST- there is Anti-matter or 'God's playdough.' As we peer inside our universe, we are imbued with the understanding that we exist inside an impenetrable ball that is but one of an indeterminate number of universes each contained within impenetrable spheres. Each sphere contains a single embryo…

For the sake of perspective, picture a clear ball, let us say about the size of a large crystal-ball. It is filled with a formless energy that appears black but is as clear as water.

(It looks black because of the surrounding blackness of the void). The ball represents our universe many billions of years in the past.

Now look closely at the energy. It fills the ball. The substance is without form, or motion, and consequently time, and at this point exists at absolute zero.

This is anti-matter, the most natural substance in existence. All that you enjoy was originally anti-matter. This, of course, includes you and me.

• SECOND - there is vibration, which must come from the outside, and somehow penetrate the impenetrable ball, much like a spermatozoa penetrates and fertilizes an egg...Before this penetration, and subsequent vibrations, nothing was happening inside the egg!

As vibration asserts itself, raising the universal temperature within the sphere, above absolute zero, anti-matter uniformly ceases to exist as anti-matter, turning instantly into rudimentary "Dark-Matter," and the creation of the first-dimension.

In other words, with a temperature increase above absolute zero, anti-matter instantly and universally transforms into dark-matter. (All that occurs within our universe is unaffected by other universes, nor does our universe affect them).

What is now fundamental matter is universally affected in that the pattern is present everywhere within the sphere of our universe. (Keep in mind that you are observing the formation of atomic particles). Also keep in mind that whenever you observe the universe, even when there is nothing but the first-dimensional space, there is ALWAYS a three-dimensional space within the energy-filled sphere. As the second-dimension accrues, it too is defined by three-dimensional space.

Energy

Before we get into various kinds of energy, please understand that there is only one energy source: *Dark-Matter*. We see it manifesting in its endless forms, from hydrogen gas clouds to magnificent waterfalls. From stars to galaxies and beyond, and of course, as you and me...

Understanding Gravity

(I discovered the following information, in the far future, and as such, might be a bit difficult to understand in your present time...which, relatively speaking, exists in the dim past).

As I understand it, at present, we exist in an anti-gravitational universe, filled with "Gravitational Energy," meaning, that a relentless tsunami of invisible energy flows from the outside to the inside of any object and down through it from all points towards its center forming a whirlpool-like gravitational well. This is the opposite of a gravitational universe, in which gravitational energy flows from the inside to the outside...The Egyptians understood this and took advantage of it through their building of pyramids...

A WAY OUTSIDE THE BOX

Trapped in the third-dimension, gravitational energy seeks a return to the first-dimension, its point of origin...

A great deal like a whirlpool, gravitational energy descends upon a suitable object from all sides flowing down through it to its center where it exits into the first-dimension. This sucking motion affects all other objects within the vicinity of its gravitational well. The bigger the well, the greater the influence. Many competing gravity-wells are also created in all suitable objects.

To better understand this, picture the earth as about the size of a basketball, in a swimming pool, positioned in the middle, halfway between the surface and the bottom. A whirlpool of water is forcing itself into the basketball, everywhere on its surface, and down through it to its center, where it is forced into another dimension. If there are other objects in the pool, they too will be attracted to the gravitational-well. This is what gravitational energy looks like as it creates gravity.

On our earth, for example, gravitational energy pushes everything on its surface towards its center. This includes you and me. Although we are in a constant state of falling, luckily our planet has filtered out enough detritus to keep us from actually falling. Instead, we experience falling as gravity...(Sir Isaac Newton started to write about this, but understandably changed his mind..).

Gravitational Energy

Let's look at the exact process gravitational energy goes through to interact with matter.

• Gravitational energy, (also referred to in this book, as Eather, and Dark Energy), interacts directly with subatomic particles in the third-dimension as *friction*. The more particles the more this energy pushes down through them and so a penny is heavier than a feather.

• Similarly, gravitational energy interacts with your physical body on these same levels. The more mass you have (the more subatomic particles) the heavier you are.

• Take earth for example, as energy returns, through the center of the earth, to the first-dimension everything else is held back. Understand that all objects in the universe, capable of gravity, filter out *everything except pure energy*. This means that our Sun, for example, started as a simple return to the first dimension. A "return, also known as a "white hole," can be any size from the largest star, to planets, moons in the macrocosm, and atomic and subatomic particles in the microcosm.

There is a periodic reversal of polarity, causing our universe to switch from a gravitational state to an anti-gravitational state. This could simply be part of the cycle in which the universe comes and goes... In a gravitational universe, nothing as we know it, could exist...

Hydrogen

Our star has filtered out everything, especially hydrogen, causing it to amass. Eventually, at a certain point, a critical amount of hydrogen accumulated and began the "fusion" process, that of converting hydrogen into helium. This, of course, brought into being the beautiful life-giving star we call Sol. (As the sun formed it was, most likely, passing through a hydrogen rich area).

I will try to clear up some confusion that may have arisen during your long slog through this tome.

Quantum Physics

Because you live in the plane of duality everything is of a divided nature. There are always two separated halves of whatever you are looking at. It is so natural to us that we seldom notice.

It is only natural that when modern science stumbled upon this strange phenomenon, they would claim it as a world-shaking discovery, *which it is*. Quantum entanglement, are two of something influencing one another at distance, is simply because they are two halves of the same thing!

James Web Telescope

The advent of the James Web Telescope has set cosmologist's on their heads. The set-in stone Big Bang is now in question??? Are we witnessing the end of an era. (Sorry Einstein…)

I predict that eventually the JWT or its ilk will encounter identical twin, or more, galaxies. This phenomenon is due to the bounce off of the outer shell of our Universe. The light close to the outer shell will bounce off of it, causing the illusion of two or more identical galaxies.

The Universal Akasha holds everything that has ever happened, in minute detail. It is like a 360-deg. camera that photographs everything on earth, and our universe, simultaneously, and is able to present any part of it upon demand, in 3d holograms, simply through a form of expectation, with which we form our external realities...

The Akasha retains the rules of the second-dimension, (that of no movement or time), yet interfaces with the third dimension due to its close proximity.

(Remember the second-dimension? It is the one where everything ever ideated is located. Cities, cars, houses, ideas, but absent people or any living thing).

The Akasha contains perfect recordings of every lifetime of every living thing, along with every non-living thing. These records are recycled in perfect harmony with present time realities as holograms.

This amazing phenomenon synchronizes your lifetime like a universal movie or series of holograms.

The Brain

Our brains are the most sophisticated instruments found on planet earth. However, it is good to keep this fact in mind, they are never more than incredible instruments.

The brain will offer answers to any question about information to which it has been exposed and does so instantaneously. It then presents the requested answers to the mind. This is where thing get a bit wonky. Because we as human beings have been taught how not to use this magnificent instrument, there is a substantial delay in the transfer, many times resulting in garbled information or even its complete loss.

The remedy to this appalling situation must begin in the first grade, and continue on through college...The system, as it stands, is producing little more than mental zombies. The problem is not with the brain, it is with the Mind. The mind is a consciousness that develops in tandem with the brain.

For the mind to function properly, there are certain steps that must be taken. First among these is receptivity. Much like a catcher in a baseball game. The mind must be receptive to the pitcher, (brain). catching every pitch.

Secondly, is for the mind to trust the brain. It is essential that the mind not only trust the brain, but that it increasingly develops the speed at which it is able to receive and understand the information. The goal is eventually to instantaneously process the information until there is little or no time lag between pitch and the catch...

Savants

It has been hypothesized that some savants operate by directly accessing deep, unfiltered information that exists in all human brains that is not normally available to conscious awareness. In some cases, savant syndrome can be induced following severe head trauma to the left anterior temporal lobe.[1] Savant syndrome has been artificially replicated using low-frequency transcranial magnetic stimulation to temporarily disable this area of the brain.[17] Wikipedia

It is apparent to me that in many cases, spectacular abilities seem to arrive when a barrier is either missing from birth or damaged due to head trauma.

Rather than whacking our little darlings in the head, I am suggesting a persistent strategy with the goal of bridging the barrier, through in depth repetitive mental exercises.

Speed Reading

Speed reading for example. I discovered a device that was constructed with a timed slider. I was able to reach temporary speeds of over two thousand words per minute, with a 95% recall. I mention this to point out that there are devices available. Online programs along this line would be of immense help, as well. Through studies, it has been found that the brain goes to sleep, due to boredom, at reading speeds of less than a thousand words per minute!

Training the mind is a lot like training a child, and so must be done early on to prevent the misdirected information that now pervades our learning facilities, from infecting these young minds.

The remedy is obvious to me, and when it becomes obvious to educators, then amazing changes will occur in humanity...

Emotions

Emotions color every corner of our consciousness. We fear becoming Spock from Star Trek if we were to lose our emotions. However, most people still use emotions learned as children. When we tire of this, we look for something better, and we find it. That you are trapped in the past, your emotions are all that you can change...

Flat emotions allow us to experience next evolutionary emotions, exchanging tantrums for bliss and universal love.

Time
What Is It, How Does It Work?

Time, as I understand it, is relative. It is dependent on there being objects in motion for comparison. Without motion, there can be no relative time, only static states. This means that for something to move from A to B, there has to be a period of time allocated for it to get there. There has to be motion for there to be time.

How fast or slow it moves can be compared to, say, something moving from C to B, as compared to A to B. Now we can compare them and estimate a relative value for time.

The most natural state for time is nonexistence, as is antimatter. Unless something happens to disturb them, they can lay dormant forever…

Past, Present Future

Time can be compared to an old-fashioned reel of film. The projector illuminates each frame one at a time, as present time.

The film is travelling from the future to the past. However, here is where it gets tricky.

If you consider that the future, for each individual, has already happened, that the future frames already exist on the film, then there develops a paradox. By this I mean, if the future is set, as on a film, then the future is actually the PAST, because it has already happened and as such, predictable.

To continue with this example, as each frame passes the present time lens, it becomes the potential future, rather than just the past. In other words, the future is stored in the past, ready for viewing when the film loop starts over, presenting again as the future/past. Just substitute hologram for film reel. This repetition is due to the tendency for any motion in the 3D to continue on, perhaps for eternity...

The above, although confusing, is how your lifetimes repeat until your oversoul returns from the actual future to reeducate you…and free you from your repeating time loop, which it had previously created, to assure that you are safely preserved.

Relative Time
How Relative Time Works.

I am sure you have noticed that if you are waiting for something to happen, time seems to flow at a glacial pace. Contrarily, if you are enjoying yourself, time seems to fly. This kind of time is relative within the framework of the human psyche. As long as there is motion our brains calculate the relativity between fast and slow. However, human time is different than, say, dogs time. Dogs exist in present time, so to them every event takes place now. There is a very small window of relativity for them.

On the other hand, for example, there is a very small window of relativity for humans compared to a being who is thousands of years old. This is why it is called relative time… To further confuse the issue, there is actually no such thing as "time," time by itself does not exist. It only comes into temporary existence as a concept used by sentient beings to make sense of their realities.

Take for example, Antimatter, that exists at absolute zero, for eternity. This is the natural state of potential matter. A state of timelessness, which is its natural or base state, where time is not even a concept. The concept of time only comes into existence when Antimatter is disturbed

Dark Energy

Dark energy, what is it and why is it important? Dark energy used to be called the Ether, or Aether.

Below Is A Description Of Ether From Wikipedia.

Ether, also spelled aether, also called luminiferous ether, in physics, a theoretical universal substance believed during the 19th century to act as the medium for transmission of electromagnetic waves (e.g., light and X-rays), much as sound waves are transmitted by elastic media such as air. The ether was assumed to be weightless, transparent, frictionless, undetectable chemically or physically, and literally permeating all matter and space. The theory met with increasing difficulties as the nature of light and the structure of matter became better understood. It was seriously weakened (1887) by the Michelson-Morley experiment, which was designed specifically to detect the motion of Earth through the ether, and which showed that there was no such effect. Wikipedia

Note: "Ether" does exhibit friction with everything having mass, as it manifests as gravity, however, this phenomenon seems to occur in the microcosm, producing friction with subatomic particles, as it passes through them, rather than with atomic particles,. (Note, Dark energy, gravitational energy, and Ether, are essentially the same...only the names are different).

Michelson-Morley

Wikipedia-

"The **Michelson–Morley experiment** was an attempt to measure the <u>relative motion</u> of the <u>Earth</u> and the <u>luminiferous aether</u>,[A 1] a supposed medium permeating space that was thought to be the carrier of <u>light waves</u>. The experiment was performed between April and July 1887 by American physicists <u>Albert A. Michelson</u> and <u>Edward W. Morley</u> at what is now <u>Case Western Reserve University</u> in <u>Cleveland</u>, <u>Ohio</u>, and published in November of the same year.[1] – Wikipedia

The experiment compared the <u>speed of light</u> in perpendicular directions in an attempt to detect the relative motion of matter through the luminiferous aether ("aether wind"). The result was negative, in that Michelson and Morley found no significant difference between the speed of light in the direction of movement through the presumed aether, and the speed at right angles. This result is generally considered to be the first strong evidence against some <u>aether theories</u>, as well as initiating a line of research that eventually led to <u>special relativity</u>, which rules out motion against an aether.[A 2] Of this experiment, Albert Einstein wrote, "If the Michelson–Morley experiment had not brought us into serious embarrassment, no one would have regarded the relativity theory as a (halfway) redemption."[A 3]:219

Michelson–Morley type experiments have been repeated many times with steadily increasing sensitivity. These include experiments from 1902 to 1905, and a series of experiments in the 1920s. More recently, in 2009, **optical resonator** experiments confirmed the absence of any aether wind at the 10^{-17} level.[2][3] Together with the **Ives–Stilwell** and **Kennedy–Thorndike experiments**, Michelson–Morley type experiments form one of the fundamental **tests of special relativity**." [A 4] – Wikipedia

The fundamental flaw with their theory was assuming that the eather had to behave like a submarine through water, or aircraft through air.

Unfortunately, Michelson-Morley assumed that the Eather could be measured. When they found that it could not, they assumed that the Eather, rather than their theory, had to be wrong. (This is me pulling my hair out..).

Dark Energy Cont.
Why Is It Important?

In the theory we are studying, dark energy fills your enclosed universe. When disturbed, it luminesces, causing an expanding radiant ball of light, out into the universe, which continues even after bouncing off of the outer barrier. The maximum speed at which it can expand is "the speed of light." *Incidentally, the speed of light can shed a lot of information about the nature of dark energy...*

In order to travel faster than the speed of light, one needs to travel via means other than dark energy. (Perhaps gravitational waves).

Conclusion

Aether was used in one of Sir Isaac Newton's first published theories of gravitation, Philosophiæ Naturalis Principia Mathematica (the Principia, 1687). Wikipedia

Newton stated that the Aether flowed down toward the earth as gravity. However, he later changed his position… (Which was perfectly understandable, considering the mind-numbing amount of information he was already releasing, as it was. He probably thought that turning gravity upside down as well, would be the straw that broke the mind of the commoner..).

VOLUME TWO

(For higher I.Q. students)

Our Universe In A Nutshell

It is important to understand that ultimately, your Universe is but a single living cell, existing in a structure of untold numbers of similar cells. When your heart ceases to beat, your universe, (cell), will dissolve back into its fundamentals. Meanwhile, as the God of your universe, your emotional attitude affects the general character of everything! If you don't like something in your universe, stop interacting with it, by ignoring it as though it doesn't exist, and it will gradually cease to exist...smiling

I will attempt to show you your universe in its simplest form. Think of the universe as a sphere. Within the sphere, there are three separate dimensions: the First, Second and Third.

The Third dimension exists in the center of the sphere, as the north-pole of a unipolar construction. It is where you live. (Refer to drawing on page 68).

The First dimension surrounds the sphere as an electron field. It is also the south-pole of the same unipolar construction.

The Second-dimension separates the First and Third dimensions. It does this by existing as a void. In addition to the void is a barrier. The barrier takes the form of a shell that completely encapsulates the void and the Third dimension.

The dynamics of a unipolar construction dictates an insatiable need to unify the two poles, that crushes anything attempting to separate them. This crushing together is the signature of Creation, and the secret to how such a prodigious amount of energy is contained in such a relatively small space...

Christ Viewpoint

The Christ viewpoint is of the internal sub-dimensions, contained within the Fifth Dimension. It is like Russian nesting dolls, where the globes are stacked dimensions, separated only by vibration. This viewpoint does not touch or include anything outside of the creative or Christ realm, with the one exception, that of the 1st dimension.

The successive globes are in the following order:

12th dimensional globe, ultraviolet, (Pisces).

11th dimensional globe, violet. (Scorpio).

10th dimensional globe, purple. (Cancer).

9th dimensional globe, indigo. (Sagittarius).

8th dimensional globe, blue. (Aquarius).

The next globe is Libra, 7th dimensional, which is green, and *the center of the spectrum.*

Being green makes it the complement of red. (Aries). The outermost globe.

The successive globes contained inside of green are each complements of those globes located as successively higher vibrational globes, outside of the green globe, as shown below

6th dimensional globe, orange yellow. (Gemini). (It's complement is blue).

5th dimensional globe, bright yellow. (Leo). (It's complement is indigo).

4th dimensional globe, orange. (Capricorn). (It's complement is purple).

3rd dimensional globe, burgundy. (Virgo). (It's complement is violet).

2nd dimensional globe, brown. (Taurus). (It's complement is Ultraviolet).

The 1st dimensional globe is infrared through red, in vibration. (Aries).

(It's complement is green, (Libra). This physical opposition of Aries and Libra is perfectly understandable when you consider that Aries is the extreme outside globe and Libra is the most central globe, and the fact that they are complements.

Aries, as the outermost vibratory shell, encompasses all other globes, and as such, is the 1st dimensional globe, *positioned between the 1st and 2nd dimensions, as a barrier, separating and delineating them.*

Below is a supplemental chart showing the order and placement of the twelve dimensions.

Key= **1** PHYSICAL, Low. **2** MENTAL, Middle... **3** SPIRITUAL High Vibrations

Each Master Sign has three sub-divisions, consisting of one of each:

1-Physical, (lowest vibration).

2-Mental, (middle vibrations).

3-Spiritual signs, (highest vibrations).

Below is the layout for Aries. Notice that each is numbered (1), denoting the lowest vibrational set, Physical.

FIRST SERIES, PHYSICAL

1-(RED) ARIES-FIRE SIGN-APRIL MASTER-PHYSICAL

(The three sub-divisions of Aries)

1-(BROWN) - TAURUS - MAY – (beginning) physical

1-DARK YELLOW - GEMINI - JUNE – (beginning) mental

1-(PURPLE) - CANCER - JULY – (beginning) spiritual

Notice how the months of the year line up perfectly.

Below is the layout for Leo. Notice they are each number (2), denoting the middle vibrational set, Mental.

SECOND SERIES, MENTAL

2-(YELLOW) LEO-FIRE SIGN-AUGUST MASTER-MENTAL

(The three sub-divisions of Leo)

2-(BURGUNDY) VIRGO - SEPTEMBER - (middle) physical

2-(Green) Libra - October - (Middle) Mental

2-(VIOLET) SCORPIO - NOVEMBER - (middle) spiritual

Below is the layout for Sag. Notice they are each number (3), denoting the third vibrational set, Spiritual.

THIRD SERIES, SPIRITUAL

3 (INDIGO) Sagittarius -FIRE SIGN-DECEMBER MASTER-SPIRITUAL

(The three sub-divisions of Sagittarius)

3 (ORANGE) CAPRICORN -JANUARY – (highest vibrations) physical

3 (BLUE) AQUARIUS -FEBRUARY- (highest vibrations) mental

3 (ULTRAVIOLET) PISCES -MARCH - (highest vibrations) spiritual

The spiritual giants of old created this.

Notice that the months line up in perfect order...And that each group of three are, physical, mental, and spiritual, in that order.

This is, in addition, aligned in perfect order with the color spectrum. It is truly spectacular how each piece fits perfectly!

Stacked Configurations Of Shells

Another way of looking at this is by visualizing a red ball, about the size of a bowling ball. If we cut the ball in half, we see eleven more shells contained within. Each shell represents another vibratory center, or chakra.

The innermost shell, and the highest in vibration, is ultraviolet, Pisces. It interfaces with the innermost void...the Sixth Dimension.

Placed in the center of the spectrum is Libra, a green shell, located between Gemini, orange-yellow, and Aquarius, all shades of blue. Libras' complementary color, or opposite, is the red outer shell, and lowest in vibration, Aries. It might seem strange at first sight, but the physical relationship between Aries and Libra is perfectly understandable when you consider Aries red as the outermost shell, and Libra , green, as the most central shell...

BLACK HOLES

Current theory on black holes

(written by AI- Copilot)

A black hole is an astronomical object with a gravitational pull so strong that nothing, not even light, can escape it. Imagine a cosmic vacuum cleaner that swallows everything in its vicinity, including any form of radiation or matter. Let us delve into the details:

1. **Event Horizon**: A black hole's "surface" is called its **event horizon**. This boundary marks the point where the velocity required to escape the black hole exceeds the **speed of light**, which is the ultimate cosmic speed limit. Once something crosses this boundary, it is trapped forever within the black hole's grasp.
2. **Types of Black Holes**:
    o **Stellar-Mass Black Holes**: These compact objects form when massive stars, typically with more than **twenty solar masses**, exhaust their nuclear fuel. The star's core collapses under its own weight, triggering a **supernova explosion** that blows off its outer layers. If the core contains more than about **three times the Sun's mass**, no known force can halt its collapse into a black hole. Stellar-mass black holes are scattered throughout our Milky Way galaxy.
    o **Supermassive Black Holes**: These cosmic behemoths weigh **100,000 to billions of solar masses** and reside at the centers of most large galaxies, including our own Milky Way. Their

origins remain mysterious, but they play a crucial role in shaping galactic evolution.

- o **Intermediate-Mass Black Holes**: Astronomers suspect an intermediate class of black holes, weighing **one hundred to more than 10,000 solar masses**, exists. While only a few candidates have been indirectly identified, the most convincing example came from the detection of gravitational waves resulting from the merger of two stellar-mass black holes in 2019.

3. **The First Black Hole Image**:

- o In 2019, the **Event Horizon Telescope (EHT)** captured an image of a black hole for the first time. This international collaboration networked eight ground-based radio telescopes into a single Earth-sized dish.

- o The image revealed a **dark circle**, silhouetted against an orbiting disk of hot, glowing matter. This supermassive black hole resides at the heart of galaxy **M87**, located about **fifty-five million light-years away**, and weighs more than **six billion solar masses**. Its event horizon extends so far that it could encompass much of our solar system and beyond.

4. **Gravitational Waves**:

- o In 2015, scientists detected **gravitational waves**, ripples in the fabric of space-time predicted by **Albert Einstein's general theory of relativity** a century earlier. These waves provide direct evidence of massive cosmic events, including black hole mergers. END

What Is Gravity?
A More Thorough Study

(Nasa's Definition)

"We don't really know. We can define it as a field of influence because we understand how it operates in the universe. Some scientists think it is made up of particles called gravitons, which travel at the speed of light. However, if we are to be honest, we do not know what gravity is in any fundamental way—we only know how it behaves.

Here is what we do know: Gravity is a force of attraction that exists between any two masses, any two bodies, or any two particles. Gravity is not just the attraction between objects and the Earth. It is an attraction that exists between all objects, everywhere in the universe. Sir Isaac Newton (1642–1727) discovered that a force is required to change the speed or direction of movement of an object. He also realized that the force called "gravity" must cause an apple to fall from a tree or allow humans and animals to live on the surface of our spinning planet without being flung off. Furthermore, he deduced that gravitational forces exist between all objects.

The effect of gravity extends from each object out into space in all directions and for an infinite distance. However, the strength of the gravitational force diminishes quickly with distance. Humans are never aware of the Sun's gravity pulling them because the pull is so small at the distance between the Earth and the Sun. Yet, it is the Sun's gravity that keeps the Earth in its orbit! Neither are we aware of the pull of lunar gravity on our bodies, but the Moon's gravity is responsible for the ocean tides on Earth."

Summary

A closer look at why "Returns," ("White Holes,") are necessary. Just as "Black holes" transport gravitational energy into the third dimension, from the first-dimension, in an anti-gravitational universe, returns allow this same energy to return to the first-dimension where it started, completing its continuing cycle as a closed system.

Then again, as pressure builds in the first-dimension, (where hydrogen and helium atoms are constantly manufactured), they, hydrogen/helium, easily flow with gravitational energy, (via black holes) into the third dimension, repeating the cycle.

IMPORTANT NOTE, Understand that the engine behind the closed system is the self-perpetuating magnetic leakage between the south and north poles, creating black holes... (There are an estimated forty quintillion black holes).

Each Return causes gravitational energy to speed up as it nears its space, much like a real whirlpool. This effects other objects in the same vicinity. For example, how the sun holds planets in its orbital grasp. To gain an even better visualization of how the universe is constructed, understand that everything in creation has the fundamental form of a hydrogen atom, the original building block.

To manage this visualization, you need to think of the physical universe in terms of only three dimensions, first, second, and the third. The Third dimension, (a combination of the first, second and third sub-dimensions), is where you live. It is the nucleus, or heart of the universe, at the center of the ball that is your universe.

Picture a ball. It is surrounded by a dense electron field, which is the south pole of a unipolar configuration. At the center of the ball is the north pole. Separating the two poles is a barrier holding the void of the second-dimension, separating the second from the first. The barrier is the illusive infrared male energy, Aries which is the complement to Libra-green. It is also the 1st dimensional infrared shell, (and barrier bifurcating the 1st and 2nd dimensions). A difference in vibration, separate the second dimension from the third...

(See page 103)

There is an unwritten law that prevents movement in the second dimension. It is a place of ideation but not motion! This law places an impossible barrier for transportation of energy and atoms from the first dimension to the third. However, gravitational energy flows unimpeded through the second-dimension, to the third, via magnetic leakage between the south and north poles. This leakage results in black holes.

The manufacture of hydrogen and helium is performed in the first-dimension, where there is concerted effort to make as many atoms as possible. Because of the unipolar structure of the ball, pressure from the south pole pushes hydrogen and helium atoms towards the center of the ball, (north pole, or third dimension), However, the barrier prevents movement of these atoms from penetrating into the second-dimension and to its ultimate goal, the third dimension.

As gravitational energy flows through the second-dimension, it forms quadrillions of straw-like structures that penetrate from the first-dimension, through the second, and into the third, following the magnetic leakage. These manifest as black holes in the third dimension. The straws are different diameters, allowing easy passage of atoms, from the first to the third dimensions. As such, energy, and atoms flow through the second dimension, without violating its laws.

As gravitational energy streams through the second and into the third dimensions, it drags with it hydrogen and helium atoms. As these atoms manifest into the creative or Christ realm of the third dimension, stars and galaxies are formed at the openings of "black holes."

Due to the unique structure of the unipolar configuration, incredible pressure, constantly pushes towards the north pole from the south pole, which forces gravitational energy, down through and out of the north pole, back to the first dimension, via "returns" Everything, not nailed down, that has mass, in the third dimension, i.e., rogue hydrogen and helium atoms for example, are gravitationally drawn into the gravity wells of returns. Since the atoms are too large to travel through a return, they pile up as detritus. When we walk around on earth, for example, we are walking on this detritus... Our sun, on the other hand, piled hydrogen and helium atoms as detritus, until a critical mass was reached resulting in the fusion process, we enjoy today...

SUPER-HUMAN KINGDOM

Humanity is about to take a step, from the Human Kingdom, into the Super-Human Kingdom...This change will evolve over the next several million years. So don't get too excited... Our early ancestors walked on all fours. They, along with all other animals, were aligned with the moon. (One side of the moon is always facing the earth – Geocentric). One day, about two million years ago, several of our earliest ancestors, the very first Homo Erectus, for some reason, perhaps continuously scampering into the ocean for protection, stood upright. This caught on, and ushered us into the human kingdom, (fifth dimension or mental planes), from the animal kingdom, (fourth dimension or emotional planes). Standing erect aligned them with the magnetic alignment of the sun and planets, rather than the gravitational alignment of the moon to the earth. Thanks to them we have walked upright ever since. This also ushered in the phenomenon of individuated human Souls...

Who/What Is God

Defining "God" is a complex task, as it varies across unfamiliar cultures, religions, and philosophies. Here is a broad overview: (Written by CoPilot AI)

1. **Religious Perspective**: In many monotheistic religions like Christianity, Islam, and Judaism, God is considered an all-powerful, all-knowing, and benevolent supreme being who created and oversees the universe. Polytheistic religions, like Hinduism and ancient Greek mythology, believe in multiple gods, each with distinct personalities, domains, and powers.
2. **Philosophical Perspective**: Philosophers have long debated the nature and existence of God. Some view God as a necessary being whose existence is required for the possibility of everything else. Others see God as an abstract concept representing ultimate reality or absolute truth.
3. **Cultural and Personal Perspective**: For many, the concept of God transcends organized religion and includes a personal relationship with a higher power, spiritual being, or the universe itself.
4. **Scientific Perspective**: Science does not delve into defining God, as the concept typically lies outside empirical investigation. Some individuals reconcile their scientific understanding with their faith, while others may see them as separate realms.

The definition of God can be deeply personal and varies widely depending on individual beliefs and experiences. End

We have covered much of what God is about, but not exactly what or who It, He, she is...I am comfortable with my thoughts on the subject, and since it is such a personal definition, I will leave it at that...

A Final Word

It is quite possible that after all of the work you have done to master the lessons and techniques, nothing worked! You found that no matter how hard or long you tried, you failed to experience the promised benefits, or even a modicum of success!

This sad result held a high probability. It is much more likely than you having spectacular results…

I mentioned earlier that this was a data dump, designed for people for many years in the future.

To master most of these lessons, I struggled for many years. For you to master them in a few hours, weeks or even a year, would be beyond spectacular! More than learning the lessons, from a purely intellectual perspective, is actually becoming what is studied, that of a God Conscious Being…This state of being is largely dependent complete mastery of emotions!

The point being that you have been given the keys to the kingdom, for you to learn and become, a little at a time, at your leisure.

If we were to compare grades in school from first grade through college, as you enter the Super-human levels, you would be in the third grade. Rather than depress you, this should make you ecstatic! Just imagine all that will be revealed to you as you progress...

There is no hurry, no time limit, no pressure. The only thing that is required from you is patience. You have the rest of your life, and beyond, to practice this. Understand that at your core, you are immortal. Now that you are part of the show, there will never be a time that you are not self-aware. You will evolve on three major levels, that of Beingness, Knowingness and Doingness. They must be held in-balance, without one overly out distancing the others. It is quite common and even necessary for knowingness to surge ahead in the beginning. However, as more and more confidence accrues, breakthroughs occur in the other two. For example, as light is shed on areas of fear, those fears dissipate and allow the student to explore further into the spiritual void.

Beingness is by far the most important element garnered. It is a measure of what you have become due to your studies and perseverance. Beingness sort of creeps up on you, noticed by your friends before you do...**beingness is the third leg of the stool.**

Anything worth mastering is going to take time, patience, and the sweat of your brow…

A LABOR OF LOVE

Please appreciate the time, sacrifice, (three divorces), and dedication, (and medication), that went into bringing all of this wonderful information here into one place for you to study as you desire. Bringing you the information was the hardest part, for without it, you would be tasked with discovering it all by yourself, a daunting task of herculean proportions, that I would not wish on anyone!

As an independent researcher, I was *not* hobbled by the current patchwork-quilt of academic theories. Nor was I humbled by research grants or oversite committees. I was as free as a bird, soaring high above the academic gridlock, uncaring about what others thought of my theories, needing neither money nor permission. It was a labor of love…

I would strongly recommend starting a study group where you and your metaphysical friends can share your labors…

Although I may have passed on, I will always be with you, here in this book, to help and guide you…please rely on me for that guidance...

Addendum

(There is, to me, a persistent awareness that we coexist with a human embryo, forming in the total galaxies and solar systems that crowd our nightly sky).

I recently had an epiphany, that we, at least, here on this planet, are the future Conscience, or mind of that embryo, evolving, in tandem, as a vanguard, destined to merge with our future host, at its birth…)

A Little Brick A Brack

It is interesting to me, that when a man and woman face each other, their creative energy is focused on procreation. However, when they face apart, back-to-back, their creative energy is focused on material considerations. To understand this concept, think of a man or a woman as but one half of a whole person. When they function together, they form a complete person...

We are the most advanced organisms on our planet. Hopefully, we will eventually outgrow our tendency to eat anything that doesn't look like us. Smiling

POEM.

He gazed upon his beloved. She was beautiful beyond compare. With her face emblazoned in the stars and galaxies, he beheld her like this for eons, content to do nothing else...

She gazed upon him, his face shining in the stars. He was God-like, his eyes blazed like diamonds, his beautiful face gazing back at her. He was, and always has been, her completeness, her beloved...

Author...

Supplemental Toning

You can experiment with toning if you care to. DO vibrates the heart center. Descending scale: DO, TI, LA, where TI vibrates the upper solar plexus and can be used in conjunction with that meditation, for calming anxiety and fear. (Below is a chart showing the various tones and the related centers).

ASCENDING SCALE
(6) LA - TOP OF THE HEAD
(5) SO - CROWN
(4) FA - THIRD EYE
(3) MI - MOUTH
(2) RE - THROAT
(1) DO - HEART
\

ESCENDING SCALE
(1) DO - HEART
(2) TI - UPPER SOLAR PLEXUS
(3) LA - LOWER SOLAR PLEXUS
(4) SO - SPLENIC
(5) FA – SEXUAL CENTER
(6) MI - COCCYX

(You can feel these individual centers vibrate as you tone).

Important Points To Remember

(Understand that you are delving into a state of being that consists of equal parts Cosmic and Christ. The Cosmic provides a static state of pure bliss while the Christ provides a pulsing magnetic state that transports bliss. Together they recreate a kind of extraordinary universal love, bliss in motion, that has only itself as a reflection...that gently and irresistibly bestows exultation, magnetically, upon all those who are receptive...they in turn, like a virus, are able to automatically generate universal love as well...And bestow it upon others).

I believe we exist inside an impenetrable ball that is but one of an indeterminate number of universes each contained within impenetrable spheres. Each sphere contains a single embryo...

As a point of interest, it is the lower etheric plane where extra-terrestrials seem to thrive, accounting for many close encounters...

HERE IS SOME INFORMATION THAT FEW, IF ANY, KNOW:

Pisces is associated with the ears and is dependent on hearing in order to learn. It must sound right. "Can't believe my ears." Even when Pisces is reading, for example, an internal voice will enunciate each word. (My personal experience).

Scorpio, as most know, is associated with the eyes. And things must look right. "Something doesn't look right." (My personal experience, Scorpio moon).

Cancer is associated with the nose. Things must smell right. "This whole thing stinks!" "something smells rotten in Denmark."

And Sagittarius. Is associated with the mouth. Things must taste, right. "Leaves a bad taste in my mouth...

--End--

Physical, Mental And Emotional Bodies, Gifs

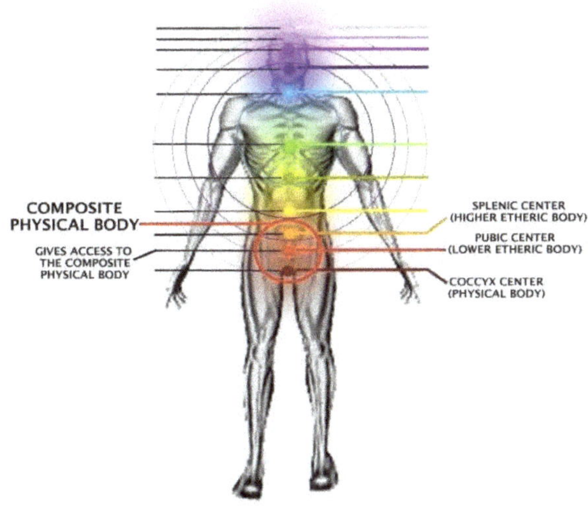

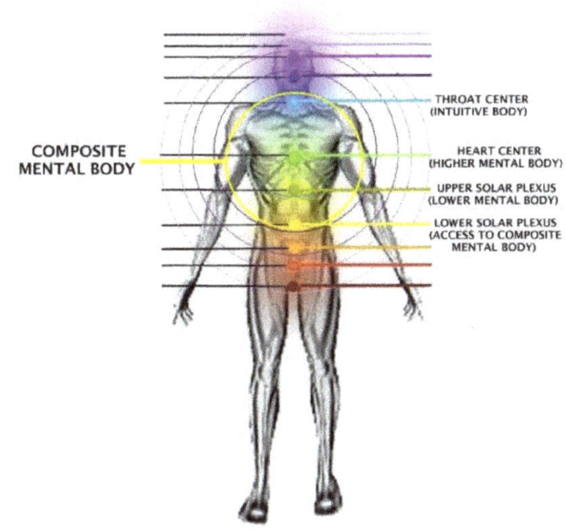

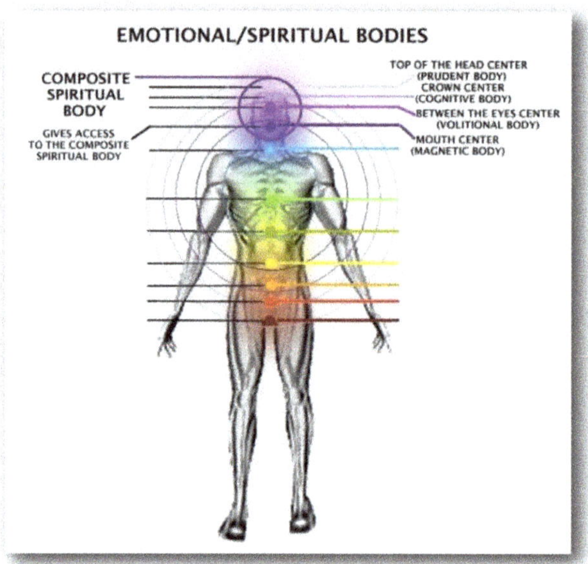
EMOTIONAL/SPIRITUAL BODIES
COMPOSITE SPIRITUAL BODY
GIVES ACCESS TO THE COMPOSITE SPIRITUAL BODY
TOP OF THE HEAD CENTER (PRUDENT BODY)
CROWN CENTER (COGNITIVE BODY)
BETWEEN THE EYES CENTER (VOLITIONAL BODY)
MOUTH CENTER (MAGNETIC BODY)